THE
LANTERN
NETWORK

Books by Ted Allbeury

THE LANTERN NETWORK
THE STALKING ANGEL
THE SEEDS OF TREASON
CHILDREN OF TENDER YEARS
NO PLACE TO HIDE
A CHOICE OF ENEMIES
SNOWBALL
PALOMINO BLONDE
THE SPECIAL COLLECTION
THE ONLY GOOD GERMAN
MOSCOW QUADRILLE
THE MAN WITH THE PRESIDENT'S MIND
CONSEQUENCE OF FEAR
THE ALPHA LIST
THE TWENTIETH DAY OF JANUARY
THE LONELY MARGINS
CODEWORD CROMWELL
THE SECRET WHISPERS
THE OTHER SIDE OF SILENCE
SHADOW OF SHADOWS
ALL OUR TOMORROWS
PAY ANY PRICE
THE GIRL FROM ADDIS
THE JUDAS FACTOR

THE MYSTERIOUS PRESS

New York • London • Tokyo

This work was originally published in Great Britain by Peter Davies Ltd.

The Mysterious Press, 129 West 56th Street, New York, N.Y. 10019

Printed in the United States of America

First U.S.A. printing: March 1989

10 9 8 7 6 5 4 3 2 1

Library of Congress Cataloging-in-Publication Data

Allbeury, Ted
The lantern network / Ted Allbeury.
p. 208.
I. Title.
PR6051 .L52L36 1989
823'.914—dc19 88-28570
ISBN 0-89296-185-6 CIP

To Spike Milligan
With Love

During and after the last war, Ted Allbeury served as an officer in the Intelligence Corps, working on counter-Intelligence duties. He is now a director of an advertising agency, and has been a farmer and a PR consultant. He now lives in Lamberhurst, Kent, with his family.

"Call no man happy until he is dead."
Cicero

PART ONE

Chapter One

It was Lovegrove, the Foreign Office liaison man, who had raised the issue under "Any other business" at the weekly meeting.

"This little fellow at the embassy reception, Walters or Waters, whatever his name is, we wondered if he shouldn't be questioned."

Paynter, the MI5 man, slowly blew out cigarette smoke with his eyes half-closed before he spoke.

"His name's Walters, James Walters. We haven't got much cause to question him. It's only an impression my chap had that the two had met before. Why don't we just keep it on file and leave it at that?"

Lovegrove fidgeted with his files and then looked up at Paynter. "My masters have a feeling in their water that he might be worth pursuing. You saw the MI6 report? Two incidents in ten days is a bit much."

Paynter brushed imaginary cigarette ash from the table top to hide his irritation: "OK, Lovegrove, we'll have a look if it doesn't take too much time."

• • •

Commander Nicholas Bailey was thirty-seven and he had had seven years in Special Branch, four years in the CID and a year with Special Patrol Group which had given him the kind of qualifications that Special Branch set store by. His French and German had been valued too, but the Oxford degree had given him a slightly Olympian attitude to routine aspects of his work that were not appreciated by some of his superiors.

He sat waiting while Paynter read the last few paragraphs of a report. Then Paynter looked up at him, pushing forward a thin file.

"This is it, Nick. There's not much to it. Bakewell was at a reception at the Polish embassy. It was a routine reception given for one of their trade missions. This chap Walters was there quite legitimately as a sub-contractor for one of their engineering suppliers. He chatted to Petrov for about ten minutes and Bakewell got the impression that they had met before, that they weren't just having cocktail-party words.

"The other bit is from the SIS man in Paris. Walters was noticed last Saturday. He visited a small gallery in Paris. Was there about half an hour and it's a place the KGB use as a dead-letter drop. The FO want us to pursue it."

"Have we got any grounds to pull him in and have a chat?"

"I wouldn't think so, there's nothing more than I've told you. You can find some excuse I'm sure, but you'll have to tread carefully or we'll get complaints from his MP and all the rest of them. It's all yours, but I shouldn't spend too much time on him. No more than you'd give to a positive vetting anyway." He stood up, hands in pockets. "I liked your report on the Russian down at Chatham. The Soviet embassy is getting a lot of stick from Moscow."

"Are they still protesting that he's not a defector?"

"When I told them that he was defecting for love of one of Her Majesty's naval aides they started back-pedalling like mad. But Moscow are insisting they issue a denial. The ambassador is making a formal complaint to the Foreign Secretary later today. That'll probably be the end of it. Anyway, let me know if I can help on this Walters thing."

• • •

Bailey had called for information from the police at Putney where Walters lived in a flat in one of the quiet streets of Victorian houses off Lower Richmond Road.

Their records showed that on two occasions in the previous four years they had had to contact Walters because of break-ins at his small factory in Wandsworth. He owned the whole house in which he lived and rented the ground floor and garden to a middle-aged couple who had been there two years. Local enquiries indicated that he was not well known and lived a very secluded life. There were few visitors to the upstairs flat and very little post. Walters shopped for food at one of the supermarkets in Putney High Street. Nobody came in to clean or cook. He appeared to have no hobbies. Two local residents recalled that a child had been injured by a car some years back and Walters had applied a tourniquet until the ambulance men came. They vaguely remembered that the local St. John Ambulance people had wanted to give him some sort of certificate but he refused it. And that was all.

• • •

Bailey had pressed the bell-push that carried the card with Walters's name. It was a Saturday morning and Bailey stood watching the children playing in the road as he waited. Then the catch on the door had opened with a buzz and he had pushed the door open and walked up the stairs.

Walters stood at the top of the stairs. He recognized him from the photographs.

"Mr. Walters?"

"Yes."

"I wonder if I could have a word with you."

"Who are you?"

"My name's Bailey. Sergeant Bailey. I'm crime-prevention officer at the local nick. I wanted to talk about your place at Wandsworth."

Walter looked intently at Bailey's face as if he might have

to describe it some time. He waved Bailey into the flat. Bailey, aware of the eyes watching him, made no attempt to look around the room. He stood until Walters had pointed to a chair at a round walnut table.

"Sit down, sergeant."

"Thank you, sir. I was checking through our records and I saw that your factory had been broken into a couple of times in the past. We didn't have a crime-prevention bloke then and I wondered if you had had any more trouble recently."

Walters stroked his hand slowly across the pile of the old-fashioned table-cloth as he looked at Bailey.

"I wouldn't call it a factory, sergeant. More a workshop. We do get break-ins about once or twice a year. They do a bit of damage but there's no cash there, no valuables. The machinery's too solid to damage."

"Is it all insured, sir?"

"Yes it is."

"You're the owner, sir, are you?"

"Yes. It's a private limited company. My accountant is the other director. He owns two shares, I own the rest. A cup of tea before you go?"

"I wouldn't say no, sir." Bailey had not missed the broad hint.

"Milk and sugar?"

" 'Fraid so, sir, both."

Bailey looked slowly round the room after Walters had gone into the kitchen. All his instincts were roused. There *was* something about the man. He was closed in. A loner. Not just anti-social but professional. And the way he looked at Bailey's face reminded him of how policemen look at suspects. There was nothing special about the room except that it was all extremely old-fashioned. But there was a feeling of tension. A feeling that his professionally casual approach was being observed, equally professionally.

Walters came back with the tea things on a tin tray and he stood as he poured out the two cups of tea. He handed one carefully to Bailey, who decided that he was going to dig just an inch or two deeper.

"What do you make at the works, Mr. Walters?"

Walters pursed his lips dismissively as he sat down. "We fabricate steel. Pipes, ducting, that sort of thing."

"Is it export stuff or the home market?"

"Mainly this country. Some of what we make goes to contractors who assemble it overseas."

"D'you have to travel abroad much?"

Bailey noticed the tightening of the mouth and the white knuckles on the handle of the tea cup.

"Very seldom."

For a moment he hesitated and then he said: "I understand that you went to Paris recently, Mr. Walters."

Walters slowly put his cup back on the saucer. Dabbed at his trousers with a handkerchief and then looked at Bailey.

"You're not from the local police are you?"

"Not all the time, sir. Would you like to see my ID card?"

Walters shook his head but stayed silent.

"We thought you might be able to help us in our enquiries."

"What about?"

"One or two things, sir. That art gallery in Paris, sir. Galerie d'aujourd'hui I think it's called. What d'you know about that sir?"

"What else did you want to know?"

"Not much, sir. Do you go to France very often?"

"Ah. I see." Walters stood up slowly. "Excuse me a moment. It's the tea. Back in a second."

There was just the slightest hesitation as Walters turned to go and it registered in Bailey's subconscious. He remembered just such a hesitation from some long ago incident, but he couldn't recall what it was about.

Bailey heard the slow footsteps as Walters walked out to the landing. Something metallic was dropped and the footsteps stopped as the something was picked up. A door handle rattled and a door was closed.

Through the net curtains at the window Bailey could see the tops of trees, the leaves that fired green of suburban summer. There were the faint cries of children playing in the street and an odd sort of silence.

And years of professional training and instinct clicked together and he ran to the toilet and put his foot against the door. It wasn't locked. It swung open easily and the stream of blood jetted over his jacket and shirt as Walters fell sideways against the wall and then slumped forward. Bailey's crêpe soles skidded in blood as he shoved Walters up to a sitting position. He felt for his heart one with one hand and for his wrist with the other. There was an old-fashioned razor on the floor between Walters's feet. But Walters was dead and the bright arterial blood from his throat was everywhere. On the walls, the floor, in the corridor, and over Bailey's sports jacket and trousers. He left bloody footprints on the linoleum and carpet as he searched for the phone. He dialled New Scotland Yard, and he was breathing heavily as he waited for a reply.

"Duty Officer, Special Branch."

"I want Murphy, quickly."

"Chief Superintendent Murphy, yes Commander."

Bailey bit back his jibe at the point of protocol that was being made and then Murphy was on the line.

"Murphy here. What is it?"

"You remember that chap Walters?"

"No. Who is he . . . oh yes. The Foreign Office thing."

"I came to his flat to suss him out a bit and he's cut his throat."

"For Christ's sake, Bailey. It's a Saturday. I want to get home. Don't play silly buggers. What is it you want?"

"That's it, sir. What I said."

There was a long pause. "Right. You stay there and I'll send a team. Don't contact the local police or doctors or anything. We'll deal with that. When you've finished there come and see me. If I'm not here come to the flat, but for Christ's sake smile at the old lady."

• • •

While he waited Bailey went over the words again and again but there was nothing that warranted Walters's action. Apart from a guilty conscience.

The doctor had taken charge of the body and the others had cleaned up the mess as far as they could. The driver had gone off with his flat keys to bring him clean clothes and he had left two of the team to keep an eye on the place until he phoned them.

The police driver had taken him to the corner of the Fulham Road where Murphy had his flat.

Murphy was not best pleased and his big body moved restlessly in the creaking wicker chair.

"But for God's sake, Nick. He wouldn't kill himself off over questions like that."

"Maybe he thought we knew more. That I was just leading up to it."

Murphy made a dismissive gesture with his big arm, orange juice slopping from his glass.

"Look. If he is innocent he doesn't kill himself. If he is guilty of something then he has a cover story. He tries it out, for God's sake. If he's an agent he doesn't give up at a couple of questions, he bluffs it out—*then,* maybe, he kills himself."

"So what d'you think?"

"God knows." He stood up and went to the phone, dialled a number and talked for ten minutes. When he came back he sat down heavily and leaned forward.

"You'd better stay with this. Find out all you can about him. Doesn't sound as though there is much, but you'd better keep going. That's what the other boys want too."

He put his hand on Bailey's knee: "But don't take too long, my boy. We've got too much real stuff to be chasing will o' the wisps."

• • •

Bailey had gone back to his place in Kensington. A small old-fashioned flat in a converted house. There was a large living-room with a dining alcove where a wall had been knocked down to open up the main room. A smallish bedroom with a single bed, an old-fashioned toilet and bathroom combined, and a small but modern kitchen.

One whole wall, and the wall under the big windows facing the mews, were lined with books on plain wood shelves. Along the top of the window bookshelves was a model railway. About ten foot of Dublo track, some realistic landscaping and a handful of model buildings. Catching the light from the window was the *Duchess of Atholl* by Hornby and a hand-made saddle-tank loco. Half a dozen pieces of rolling stock were lined up near the control box.

He had put in the railway layout a few months after Patsy died. Until then it had been a condition of his access to Johnny that "the woman named" should not be present when the boy was with him. When things were particularly hopeless Patsy had sometimes gone to the cinema so that he and the boy could come back to the flat. Otherwise it had to be that dreary round that divorced fathers know so well. The Science Museum, the Natural History Museum, the Kensington Odeon, football or cricket in the park. However much you loved the small child, seven-year-olds run out of conversation inside half and hour, and if the subject of how they live for the rest of the week is taboo the Saturday outings are grindingly low-key. It's not possible to explain to a child that your desperate need to see him isn't really represented by this sad charade. There is so much you cannot say and you sit in the car to talk the last five minutes before you take him to the gate. The solicitor's letter said "and when returning the child of the marriage Mrs. Bailey would prefer you not to enter the premises or garden." And the small boy climbs the steps and waves and knocks, and you start the engine and drive away from the house you once lived in, through familiar roads back to the new life that never seems quite secure.

As Bailey sat with a cup of coffee and a sandwich he thought about Walters. He felt no remorse about the man's death. He would have prevented it if it had been possible, but as much out of the need to complete the enquiry as out of human concern. Bailey, for all his romanticism, was a professional. He was in a business where people died or were killed, and if you identified or dwelt on the effect on others of the death you would probably go mad. You'd certainly be no use in the job.

He went back in his mind over the questions and Murphy was right. If Walters was a normal business man there was no reason why he should kill himself and the questions would not have made any difference. There was no law against going to Paris any time you wanted and hundreds of quite innocent people would visit the gallery without knowing that it was a dead-letter box for the KGB. That was probably why it was chosen. And if he was being used positively by the KGB, there again, like Murphy had said, he'd have a cover story or he'd just bluff it out; it wouldn't be difficult at that stage. And if he were really involved with the KGB he would have been trained and he'd have enjoyed the challenge. Maybe it was something to do with Walters' business life. Tax frauds or smuggling sterling to France. But if you were smuggling cash it wouldn't be to France. The French were busy smuggling their frances out to Switzerland. The only other area was sex, perhaps combined with blackmail. He'd bear that in mind during his enquiries.

Bailey looked at his watch and then reached for the phone. He dialled and waited. He recognized her voice. Once upon a time he would have felt elated but these days it emptied his stomach.

"Who is it?"

"It's me, Jane. About tomorrow and Johnny."

"I'm afraid it won't be convenient."

"Why not?"

"Your day is Saturday. He was bitterly disappointed when you called this morning."

"It was work I'm afraid. But you agreed that tomorrow would be OK."

"Things have changed. It isn't convenient."

"Just an hour maybe?"

"I'm afraid not."

"Perhaps I could speak to him now and explain."

"He's not here. He's next door."

"OK. Thanks, Jane."

"By the way, and I have asked you before, I'd prefer you to call him Jonathan. Johnny's so common."

He sat there in the failing light. She enjoyed having this power over him. The visits cancelled at the last minute. The conditions, the righteousness bestowed by the courts. The petty thrusts that too easily pierced his armour. He dialled another number.

"4301."

"Is that Jack?"

"Yes, who's that?"

"It's Nick. Nick Bailey. Is Johnny over with you?"

"Yes, he's with the boys."

"I'd like to speak to him if that's convenient." There was a pause.

"I'm afraid I can't do that, old man."

"Why not?"

"Skipper's orders. Jane mentioned that you might call. Says it's not on, because of the order of the court."

"That's nonsense, Jack. The court order doesn't cover such things."

"No can do, friend. Them's my orders."

"OK. Thanks."

He wondered what Patsy would have been like if they had had a child and had split up. But he knew the answer. Patsy was a woman, not just a female.

• • •

The autopsy was unrevealing. Extensive X-rays indicated a healed lung scar that could have been a tubercular infection that had gone untreated. There were bone fractures that appeared to have knitted together without medical treatment. There were burn scars that were very faint on various parts of the body and an enlarged spleen that would have given trouble if the man had lived a few more years. The age of the dead man was estimated as between fifty-five and sixty and there was a handwritten note from the examiners stating that the man had been healthy and fit, but at some time had been involved in either a serious road accident or an industrial accident. The badly knitted fractures in arms, legs, feet, hands and ribs were at least thirty years old and had not received medical treatment at the time.

Bailey went first to see Walters's accountant, a Mr. Slansky, whose office was in Tooting. To his surprise Slansky was a youngish man in his early thirties, fresh-faced and cheerful.

"Any idea of why he did it, Mr. Bailey?"

"I was hoping you might be able to tell me something."

Slansky pursed his lips and leaned back, swivelling in his chair. "I've known him for years, but I knew very little about him."

"What about the business itself?"

"It makes money. He draws about five thousand a year as a salary and a couple of thousand out of the net profits."

"Has he got a lawyer?"

"Not that I know of."

"And who will own the business now?"

"I suppose the Public Trustees Office will take over until they find a will. It's a miracle how claimants appear in these cases."

"How did you meet him?"

Slansky closed his eyes in concentration. "I don't really remember. Maybe he was recommended to me." Then he leaned forward. "I've got it. He knew my old man, they met at a chess club somewhere. But I don't think they were more than acquaintances."

"What about women?"

Slansky shrugged. "He never spoke of any women friends. He didn't have friends you know. It wasn't that he was unfriendly. He just didn't need people. Didn't need to talk either. Just got on with things."

"Could I meet your father?"

"He's dead. Last year."

"Who's in charge at the works now?"

"I've made the foreman temporary manager. He's a good chap. Very loyal."

• • •

Arthur McGuiness had one of those smooth raw Scots faces that go with long service in the Regular Army and shaving in cold water. He stood in his brown overall coat in the tiny office, looking through the window at the workshop as he spoke.

"No, I wouldn't say we were friends. It was master and man and no' the worse for that. He was OK."

"Did he understand the manufacturing side?"

"Och aye, there was no job in the workshop that he couldna' do better himself."

"What were his interests outside the business?"

McGuiness's watery blue eyes looked at him with surprise.

"He was ma boss, man, I didna' mind his business, and he didna' mind mine."

"Was there anything odd about him? Any peculiarities?"

"Aye, he was a good boss."

"Did he ever talk politics?"

McGuiness laughed. "He didna talk, mister. He was a doer not a clacker."

"Any regular visitors?"

"Just the usual. Salesmen and suppliers."

"Girls or women?"

McGuiness looked annoyed. "The wee man was in his late fifties. Well past that sort of game."

Bailey looked across the shop floor. "Any foreigners work here?"

"Two Welsh and one Pakistani."

He made a note of McGuiness's home address and left.

• • •

Bailey had searched Walters's flat carefully and professionally. There was not only nothing to connect its late owner with spying or the KGB, but there was nothing that connected him with anything. Bailey had heaped the few personal things on the dining-table.

There was a current British passport nearing the end of its validity. Two or three French immigration stamps in it from five years back. All showed entry at Paris except one, and that was for Bordeaux. There was nothing more recent. The full details on the passport gave his name as James Fuller Walters. Born South Croydon, Surrey, 1 November 1919.

There were three books on playing chess, Dr. Spock on bringing up children, a thick green-bound Machinery Handbook, a small set of drawing and tracing instruments in a velvet-lined case that was well made and fairly ancient. There was a small red-covered cash book that showed page after page of minor household expenditure on food and oddments. A full-sized Staunton chess set in ivory in an elaborate ebony case with a newish chess-board and a cheap miniature chess set that was all plastic and paper. There was a large brown envelope with a couple of dozen cuttings from newspapers. Most of them were small classified advertisements by individuals offering things like pianos or watches for sale. There were two large cuttings, both faded. The first was of a group of people standing at a war memorial and the second was a small item from a newspaper about Wandsworth Metal Fabrications, a local firm who were contributing to the export drive. It was Walters's company.

There was a bundle of cashed cheques with two bank statements. One was for a deposit account that held £20,104 and the second was a current account that showed a credit balance of £1,401.75. The banked cheques seemed to be routine payments but the Special Branch accountancy experts could check those over.

The place was so neutral, like a superior prison cell or a monk's retreat. No reading matter, not even a magazine or a newspaper, everything clean and in place, and no hint of the personality who had lived there. In the kitchen there had been no more than a week's supply of anything and the china and utensils were for maximum of two.

There had been very little in Walters's clothes that he was wearing when he died. The appointments in the diary had been checked. They were all business appointments.

He had found the contractor who had invited Walters to the reception at the Polish embassy. Mr. Silver was helpful, but he didn't add much.

"We'd sent him invitations before but he didn't go. He wasn't that kind of man."

"You invite all your sub-contractors to these things?"

"Usually. Depends on what the embassies say. It's their party, not ours."

"And this time they suggested that sub-contractors should be invited?"

"I expect so. We shouldn't have asked him otherwise."

"Well thanks, Mr. Silver. If you think of anything that might have caused this perhaps you'll contact me."

• • •

Bailey had left the Palmers, who lived in the flat below Walters, until last.

Palmer was a middle-grade official at the local authority, working in their housing department. His wife was a typist at an architect's office near Putney Bridge.

Palmer was in his forties and his wife was about thirty. Bailey's check through the local police only showed a routine pattern. One traffic offence, one distubance with a neighbour over a bonfire. Well thought of by the local authority, and due for a promotion when the economic climate improved.

Bailey was offered, and accepted, the ritual cup of tea, and when they had all had a sip or two he got going.

"You know about the tragedy upstairs?"

"We saw what it said in the local paper. I gather you found his dead body and it looked like he might have killed himself."

"We're pretty sure he did commit suicide and that means we have to make a few routine enquiries."

"Of course." Palmer pulled down his maroon sweater as if preparing for anything that might happen.

"Did he have any visitors, any friends?"

Palmer looked quizzically at his wife and then at Bailey.

"Apart from people delivering things or reading meters nobody ever came. We often talked about it. We invited him down here frequently. He only came two or three times."

"What sort of man was he?"

"He was a nice man, very quiet, very gentle." Mrs. Palmer held her husband's hand as she spoke. And her husband took up her statement. "We sometimes wondered if he'd got some problem. We used to hear him walking up and down late at night. It wasn't a nuisance or anything like that, not noisy, but it made the light swing a bit." Palmer leaned forward as if he were gaining confidence from talking. He turned to his wife: "D'you remember the gramophone record time?" She nodded and looked at Bailey. "We've had many arguments about it. The first time he came down here we'd just had a new record-player and I played him some records. And there was one that he asked us to play twice." She smiled. "I always said that he'd had tears in his eyes when he heard it. John says I imagined it. But I didn't." She ended defiantly.

"What was the record?"

"It was a song. In French. We've still got it. I'll check. I couldn't pronounce it anyway."

She went over to a shelf and her husband poured more tea while they waited. "Here we are," she said, walking over to him and handing him the record. It was a "78" of Josephine Baker. On one side she was singing "La Petite Tonkinoise" and on the other "J'ai deux amours." Bailey looked up smiling. "Can you remember which side it was that interested him?"

"No, but I'd recognize it if I heard it. And John would, wouldn't you, John?"

Bailey held out the record. "Try that side first." The record player was opened, switched on and she lowered the arm on to the record. After a few bars they said almost in unison, "That's it." And the sharp birdlike voice of Josephine Baker fluted the words as only she could: ". . . mon pays et Paris . . . j'ai deux amours . . ." They were not interested enough to play it all through but the few bars had touched a button in Bailey's mind. Touched but not pressed.

There had been nothing more that he had learned from the Palmers but he had left them a phone number where they could contact him.

• • •

There had been other things he had to do and it was three months later that he had been asked to the weekly liaison meeting of the various security agencies.

Bailey was only "in attendance" and he had sat in the outer office for over an hour waiting for them to reach the point on the agenda headed "Walters, J. F.—security investigation."

They were still talking about the previous case as he settled himself at the table with his file. It was Paynter's turn to chair the meeting and he nodded in Bailey's direction.

"Commander Bailey has been doing the check on the little chap. As you know he cut his throat and that's about the only indication we have had that he might have been doing something naughty. I think we may have frightened him into it. He was a quiet little nonentity and he must have panicked. If he *had* been in 'the business' he wouldn't have been so frightened or so stupid. I think we can close the file, but let's hear what Bailey's got to say."

Bailey opened his file and looked briefly round the table as he spoke.

"Gentlemen, I've been able to produce very little on this man. I was on the case exclusively for five weeks and I have spent time on it sporadically for a further three months. All the information I have gathered merely supports my own opinion the Walters was a quiet, inoffensive little man who lived a quiet life running his business. No visitors, no friends, a self-contained man. He had only been to the one embassy reception although he had been invited to several." He leaned back in his seat, pushing the file to one side: "I should have to spend a lot of time to get any more details. I'm pretty sure it's not worth it."

It was Lovegrove who leaned forward. "The MI5 man only said that he felt that Walters and Petrov had met before. It was just a professional instinct. Do you feel any such doubts?"

Bailey sat up in his chair "I suppose I do. Here was a man of fifty-eight or whatever he was. He didn't do *anything*. Just went to work and came back again. No friends. No acquaintances even. Absolutely inoffensive. An ideal citizen. Barely noticed by anybody. No political connections, no anything. A grey mouse."

"No women or anything like that?" asked Lovegrove.

"Nothing. I suppose it's the nothingness that challenges me, that makes me suspicious."

"Suspicious of what?"

"I really don't know."

Paynter waited to see if any of the others wanted to speak, but there were no takers.

"Can I take it, gentlemen, that we agree that we can close the file?"

Lovegrove nodded his head slowly as he fiddled with a pencil. He looked at Paynter then at Bailey. "Maybe we don't close it. Let's see if anything else comes up some time."

Paynter looked at Bailey: "Agreed, Commander?"

"Agreed, sir."

• • •

"I think I liked the old Lion House better."

"Why's that?"

The small boy screwed up his nose and frowned.

"It was easier to see them than here. And it's all muddy. Lions don't live in muddy places."

"They can spread themselves around more here."

"Daddy, why do they call lions, lions?"

"It's just their name. Like dogs are called dogs. Like you're called Johnny."

"Mom says my name's not Johnny it's Jonathan."

"When you're with me you're Johnny."

"Sort of like Jekyll and Hyde?"

Bailey laughed.

"Sort of. What d'you want to see next?"

"The snakes."

"I thought you didn't like snakes."

"I don't. But I like to look at them."

"Let's go and have a cuppa first."

"Can I have coke instead?"

"Sure."

They sat in the restaurant and Johnny fed crumbs to a sparrow that flew down to the table. Without turning his head the small boy said, "Why don't you live with us any more?"

"I thought your mother had explained."

"She did. But I don't understand."

"What don't you understand?"

"She said you love another lady."

"That's true."

The blue eyes looked up at his face: "But Mummy said that lady died."

"She did."

"So why don't you come back to us?"

"I don't think your mother would want that."

"Do you?"

"I don't think so, Johnny. It's hard to explain to a small boy."

"Mummy said the trouble with you is you're a romantic."

"Maybe she's right."

"That's kissing, isn't it?"

Bailey smiled. "I guess so."

"And Mummy doesn't like that sort of thing does she?"

"Have you finished your coke?"

"Yes."

"Let's go and see those snakes then."

• • •

It was nearly eight o'clock when Bailey got back to Kensington. He'd parked his car and taken a taxi to St. James's Park. He got out at the Buckingham Palace circle and walked to the bridge and then down to the Passport Office. A Russian from the Trade Mission had defected that morning and he was to do the preliminary interview.

PART TWO

Chapter Two

He sat in the hedge with the others, looking up to where the full, white moon hung in an almost cloudless sky. The lights which made an inverted "L" were in place but unlit, and his thumb lay across the button on his torch that would give the identification signal to the plane.

They had laid out a line that would give the pilot a cross-reference from the river that he could pick up at Mauroille. If it hadn't been for London's instructions the plane could have come straight in, but Baker Street must be in a touchy mood, they had insisted that before the pick-up there would be a check on the S-phone. The Gestapo and the Sicherheitsdienst had been blitzing the Special Operations Executive resistance networks in the last five weeks and London was taking no risks. With the S-phone you could talk from plane to ground by microwave and the voices would be as clear as a local telephone call. Clear enough to pick out an alien accent or the constricted throat that came from a Luger at the back of a man's head.

His left hand held the phone to his ear and he tried not to

think of all the loose ends he had left lying around at Brive. Local legend said that the village had got its name of Brive-la-Gaillarde from putting on a brave face over centuries of sieges. But the present community of small-holders and fruit-growers, after three years of harassment by the Germans, were now very near the end of their tether. He closed his eyes and bent his head in the direction of the faint sound. A few seconds later the radio at his ear crackled and he could hear the speaker clearly. "Asylum calling Trojan. Can you hear me?"

"Trojan to Asylum, I can hear you clearly."

"Give me four cinemas in Brum, Trojan."

"Christ!—The Gaumont, Steelhouse Lane; the Plaza, Stockland Green; the Star, Slade Road and the Forum in town. I can't remember the street."

"And who wears claret and blue?"

"Aston Villa."

"OK, Trojan. Put the lights on in two minutes . . . from *now*."

Parker switched off the radio-phone and flashed his torch twice and as the men moved to the lights their figures cast long shadows on the moonlit grass. As the lights went on they could see the dark shape of the Lysander, its wide wings wagging as the pilot fought the cross-wind. He pressed the torch button—dot dash dot dash. Then the small plane was lost below the blackness of the trees, and moments later it was bumping and bouncing across the field.

Parker exchanged no farewells but ran forward and took the short ladder that was already half-way down to the ground. There were two passengers; he could see that one was Fredericks and the other was a dark man. He was a replacement radio operator for a reseau in Paris. He helped him down with the two heavy cases and then went up the ladder and pulled it up behind him, ducking as the pilot closed the canopy. The engine revved and he barely had time to sit in the seat at the back of the pilot before they were moving. They had left the rear machine-gun mounting in place and there was scarcely room for both him and Fredericks. The sky slanted alongside him, they were airborne and banking in a wide turn.

They had flown south of Bordeaux and then out to sea. He guessed that they would be landing at Tangmere, they wouldn't have petrol enough for Tempsford.

He had been asleep when they touched down and Fredericks shook him awake. There was a Luftwaffe attack on the airfield at Ford and they were expecting a diversion raid at Tangmere. He remembered being shoved into a big black Humber and he had slept until they were going through Streatham. It was just getting light and there were hoses across the main road. They were diverted round the common and he saw the still-smoking ruins of several houses and a pub. There were buildings still burning at Clapham.

They had gone over Westminster Bridge and he saw the signs to the Air Raid Shelters. The sun was out as they swung round the back of Selfridges and a few minutes later he was at Orchard House.

Fredericks had carried his kit up the stairs where Foster was waiting for them. He held out his hand smiling but Parker had noticed the tired eyes and the effort of smiling.

"Glad to see you back, Charles. How'd you feel?"

"Skint."

"Freddie's fixed you a bed at his place for today and when you've rested we'll talk." His hand brushed at his hair diffidently. "There are just a couple of quickies, Charles."

Parker nodded: "One's Bordeaux, yes?"

"Yes. What d'you think?"

"I think it was penetrated by the SD months ago. Take it from me that it's insecure."

"Feeling, Charles, or a fact or two?"

Parker took a deep breath and then closed his eyes as he spoke, as if he wanted to exclude everything but the words. "Feelings, yes, and I would bet on Grandclement as the one. Facts, yes. The SD and the Gestapo have been hitting all the reseaux for two months solid. From Bordeaux to La Rochelle up the coastal strip the Germans are thick on the ground. SD, Gestapo, Feldgendarmerie, Milice—the lot, but they haven't picked up a single operator. They picked up Grandclement and held him for four days. When he came out the story was that he'd fooled them. But since then they've picked up seven caches of arms and explosives. In my opinion he did a deal, and my people have been told to break off all contact with his group."

"We're still getting normal radio from his group."

"I'd like to see it."

"And so you shall."

"What was the other question?"

"Would you trust Devereux?"

"My Devereux?"

"Yes."

"With my life."

"OK, Charles, we'll talk again when you've had a sleep."

• • •

Parker had almost forgotten that he was back in safety and had got into the divan bed still fully clothed. As he got out and slowly undressed he looked out of the window. All he could see were pots of geraniums and other greenery that stood at the sides of the basement steps. Devereux would be preparing the explosive about now for the raid on the railway-sheds at Tulle that night. If they got the round-house it would stop supplies to the car-engine factory for at least four weeks, but even a couple of shunting locos would be a worthwhile prize.

As he settled under the blankets he realized that he stank. He hadn't had a bath for a month. He wondered what Foster and Fredericks wanted.

• • •

Charles du Puy Parker had been born in Birmingham on the last day of October 1918. His father, a sergeant in the Regular Army, had died when the boy was three and he had been brought up by the widow in the small terraced house in Victoria Road, Aston. An area given up to skilled artisans and small enterprises. His mother was French and she had met the man who was to be her husband when they had brought him into the hospital in Bruges where she was a nurse. He was a gentle man, with a voice that talked to her as some men talk to highly-strung thoroughbreds, coaxing and slow, sure and self-confident. But it had been three months before he had spoken. The gas that had burnt his lungs had paralysed his throat, and he had lain still and silent with the rubber tube projecting from the incision at the base of his throat. Her parents had liked him although they regretted that he was English, but as he had joined the army from an orphanage there were no English relatives to please, and they had married in Paris when he was honourably discharged, with a pension of seven shillings a week. That was in August 1916.

He had gone back to his old job as a tool-maker, but after six months it was clear that he would not survive in the dirt and stench of a factory, and he had taken on hourly work as a jobbing gardener. But the fogs of the next winter had kindled again those terrible fires in his lungs. He was not a man to complain but the pale, drawn face and the blue round the mouth and eyes told the story clearly enough for those who cared to notice.

On Armistice Day he had been well enough to get out of bed and when he was able to get about again the baby had brought him great joy, and slowly he seemed to mend. So well indeed that the man cared for the baby while the woman earned their keep cleaning offices and other people's homes. The man was a regular visitor with the pram to the shops in Aston Road, and there would often be a casual hand stretched out to help him push the precious load back up the hill. The gasping, wheezing breath, and the bent back were noted without comment. By the time the baby was a toddler there was sometimes a tram-ride to Handsworth Park. The small boy found his father's company easier than his mother's. His father never scolded him, just smiled and picked him up in loving arms. It was many years later when the boy realized that his father hadn't talked because of the pain raging in his chest.

It was in the spring of 1922 that his father had died. He had seemed to withstand the winter well and with the sunny days of April there had seemed to be no problem. When the small boy had awoken that night he was not sure whether his mother was laughing or crying. When he was upstairs in bed it was not always easy to tell. He had made his way in the darkness down the steep narrow stairs, and saw that his mother was standing in the small parlour with her arm round his father's shoulders. His father's head rested on his right arm as it lay angled on the green table cover. There was blood from his mouth across his pale white hand and it shone on the pile of the chenille cover. His mother's face was pressed to his father's cheek as if she were trying to persuade him to hear her. When she saw the small boy in his pyjamas she stood up, wiping her eyes, and she said

"Il est mort, ton père, il est mort. Il ne reviendra jamais, nous serons toutes seuls."

And the tears had fallen again the next day when he had stood holding her hand as the doctor and neighbours came to do their duty. He could remember the procession through the gates at Witton Cemetery but he had never remembered the service or the burial.

At home his mother spoke only in French, and from time to time relatives from Paris and Lyons and Poitiers came to visit, and she was complimented on his accent and fluency. His accent in English was unmistakably Birmingham, and between school and home he had two different and separate lives. As a young man he had sometimes felt as if he brought back news from the outside world to a besieged prisoner. His mother lived in a world still inhabited by his father. She talked to her ghost in the French that he would not have understood were he alive, and her only concession to his death was her constantly used, "Ton père disait toujours . . ." As he grew up he smiled sometimes at yet another Montaigne-like aphorism that his father was supposed to have said. There was no intention to deceive. The attribution was made with love, and the imparted advice was meant to help a young man in his life.

When World War II had started Charles Parker was an engineer with an agricultural engineering company on the rural periphery of Birmingham, and by February 1940 he had been called up. After his basic training he had been posted to a Royal Army Service Corps transport depot and four months later he had been interviewed in a tatty little office in a Ministry block in Westminster. The thin man whose eyes were always half-closed against the smoke of his cigarette had asked him questions, and had not seemed over-impressed with his answers. The fact that the interview had been in French had been its own small clue, and the thin man's accent had been outrageously of "le seizième."

A week later he had been posted to Wanborough Manor just outside Guildford, and there he had learned the basics of the arts and crafts that the Special Operations Executive required of its alumni. The report from the training staff had not been over-enthusiastic. It praised his courage and initiative but found him lacking in emotional qualities which they surmised might make him a loner rather than a leader. The report from the commando school at Arisaig had given an almost opposite assessment. Rating his leadership high but doubting his physical stamina. There was a suspicion expressed that he might even have "cut corners" on a map-reading exercise. It was one thing to be taught how to stalk an adversary and knife him silently with your hand over his mouth, but to deceive your instructors to avoid an unpleasant night exercise was immoral. "Cutting corners" for the warriors of Arisaig was the same as cheating, but for the officers who ran SOE from the gloomy rooms at St. Ermin's Hotel, men who "cut corners" were doubly welcome. They "cut corners" themselves, when they could, against their natural enemies. Their natural enemies being the Army, the Navy, the Royal Air Force, the weather, the Free French, a number of ministries, and the Chiefs of Staff Committee. But with Winston Churchill as its godfather SOE survived the onslaughts of those who wanted to destroy it.

By the time Parker had finished his parachute training and the months at the house near Beaulieu, SOE was ensconced in Baker Street and it was there that he had had his final briefing. Their only worry was that he had never lived in France. His French would pass him as a Frenchman albeit a little old-world in some of his expressions, but language alone doesn't make a Frenchman, and on that score they cautioned him against taking unnecessary risks.

They had dropped him and Devereux, his radio operator, just south of Clermont-Ferrand and the reception committee had taken them to the priest's house at Vic-le-Comte. They had moved down to the Corrèze the next day and Charles du

Puy Parker had successfully held together a reseau of men and women who came to control the whole area of the Corrèze.

All the training staffs had been right about Parker. He *was* a loner, but a loner who cared for his men. He did lack stamina, but living off the country in Unoccupied France called for a pacing of the spirit and body that only those conscious of their shortcomings could contrive. His men died because, with largely improvised equipment and inadequate resources, risks had to be taken. They were calculated risks and sometimes the calculations were wrong. But none of Parker's men had been broken or turned by their Gestapo or SD captors. They were Frenchmen and they had known the risks.

Parker had become something of a legend for his success and ability to harass the Germans and yet keep his men alive, and SOE in Baker Street thought that he could be better used. In addition, it was their experience that legendary leaders became prime targets for the Germans' security organizations, and when the legend went in the bag, fifty or sixty others could be on their way to Belsen or Dachau with him.

When Foster and Fredericks had hinted at a new assignment to Parker the next day, there had been none of the protests that they had expected. If that was what they chose to do, he seemed to say, then they must get on with it. They had not told him what his new responsibilities would be and he hadn't asked. He had had a week's refresher course at Arisaig, and amongst other things he had learned a new way of killing a man without making a noise. His medical check-up had indicated incipient anaemia and he'd been given a series of injections and sent on down to Beaulieu.

They had given him a farm cottage on the estate at Beaulieu and he had been inserted on a day-to-day basis into several of the groups under training. Never quite certain whether he was pupil or instructor. They had used him on the "how to avoid a tail" exercises that were mounted in the unsuspecting Southampton streets, and when he and two others had been arrested by the police in Bristol they had seen his cover-story stick so well that he had been released after four hours with a railway ticket to Southampton. The other two, however, had been taken apart so efficiently by the local CID that they had to refer the police to the duty officer at Beaulieu.

Foster and Fredericks had come down at the end of the first week, and on the Sunday evening they had told him about his new task.

• • •

It was Foster who led off, and Charles Parker had listened carefully.

"We want you to go back again—not to the Corrèze but to the Dordogne—the triangle of Angoulême—Limoges—Périgueux. By the way, did you take a W/T course in 1940?"

"Yes, but I haven't used a radio in the field."

"We'll give you a refresher course while you're here. But we'll be sending a W/T operator in with you. There's the nucleus of a reseau in the area already but it's up to you whether you keep them or send them back. We want you to do what you've done in the Corrèze—sabotage, post us on troop movements, and this time we want you to liaise with the Free French and other French authorities—we'll give you their backgrounds. You'll still be in overall charge of the reseau at Corrèze and the group at Limoges will take your orders too. We want a good solid controlled area so that when the time comes there will be an army across the main roads that can harry even major German units when they start moving them about. There's one other thing that we want you to do but you'll get separate instructions on that from Fredericks. You'll be in this country for at least a month and we've planned a series of refresher sessions for you. There are new weapons and new explosives techniques that will be useful for you. Any queries?"

"Who's my radio operator?"

"She'll be down tomorrow. Fredericks will hand her over. If you don't approve you'll have to give us your views by this time next week, good radio operators are pretty thin on the ground at the moment."

The weeks had gone by and Parker had absorbed the new training, and in the evenings he had pored over the maps of his new area and read the reports on the SOE groups at Limoges and Périgueux.

CHAPTER THREE

The winter sun was slanting through the side windows, painting the stone fireplace a golden red and lighting up the dust on the highly polished floor. It was Parker's last night in England before they dropped him back in France the next day, and he read the instructions again as he sat at the small table.

For Captain Charles Parker, organizer of LANTERN 7.12.43.

Operation Instructions No F67

Operation	:	LANTERN
Field Name	:	Charles
Name on papers	:	Charles Chaland

1. Information

Our detailed discussions about the possibility of your returning to France to assemble a reseau in the area Angoulême—Périgueux—Limoges and co-ordinate its activities with the reseau at Brive-la-Gaillarde indicate that in your view there is nothing to prevent you carrying out this mission.

We have discussed with you supplies of arms and equipment that you indicate are essential to your task and these will be dropped to your instructions, weather permitting.

Particular attention will be paid to the sabotage of all communications, including rail and telephones.

It is important that you inform us of the situation with other groups which are not part of "F" section. Any contact with other groups will be limited personally to you. Your liaison will be for information not operation.

2. Intention

(a) You will return to the Field by parachute drop together with your W/T operator as soon as weather permits.

(b) You have been given details of the situation in your area, including suitable areas for supply drops.

(c) We have described the system of BBC messages for transmission of orders for activity on D-day.
The following are the messages for your activity:
1. For communications targets
(a) Les lauriers son coupés.
(b) Il était un roi d'Yvetot.
2. For military targets
(a) Les absents ont toujours tort.
(b) L'Italie est une jambe.
3. (a) Le nez retroussé l'air moqueur.
(b) J'ai ta main dans ma main.

3. Administration

It has not been our policy to encourage the formation of large groups. Your operation is an exception, and we require you to exercise extreme caution in pursuing your objectives. If at any time it is your judgement that the overall command by you of the reseaux is proving insecure or dangerous, you will inform us immediately.

4. Finance

You will take with you to the Field the sum of 750,000 francs and you will inform us as soon as possible what your future financial needs are likely to be.

The simple, unexaggerated words only emphasized the incongruity of sitting in the sunlight in a peaceful English cottage, reading the words of quiet, ordinary men who had in mind that electricity pylons, railway tracks, telephone exchanges and bridges would be better destroyed than used by the enemy. Almost certainly people would die because of those words, and most of them would be French people.

He copied out the BBC codes without their references and put a match to the order, and by habit he pounded the order to a grey mess in the washbasin before he pulled out the plug and let the water run for a few minutes.

Locking the cottage door behind him, he walked across to the radio section. The girl was waiting for him and half an hour later he was edging the MG up the hill in Winchester. They had sat drinking a beer in the almost empty pub and the girl had tried to hide her tension. On the way back he had stopped the small car, the moon was almost full and there was the sparkle of frost on the road ahead. He turned to look at her. Antoinette Cousteau was very pretty and this was probably the first frost she had ever experienced in her life. She was a Seychelloise from Mahé and the brown eyes and light brown skin glowed with health and fitness.

"Are you scared, 'Toinette?"

Her head turned quickly and the brown eyes looked carefully at his face. "I'm afraid so."

"The drop, or what comes after?"

She laughed softly. "Just this minute I'm scared of everything. What was my report like?"

"The radio part was exceptionally good. I think they wanted to hold you as an instructor."

"And the rest?"

"Not bad. A suggestion that you were over-emotional."

The big eyes looked at him quickly: "And you disagreed?"

He half laughed. "No, I agreed. Most of my good people are emotional. I insisted that you were ideal for my operation and Baker Street agreed too."

"It must have been that bastard with two names who gave an unfavourable report."

He laughed. "You mean Miles-Hampton?"

"Yes."

"He's first-class really. You've got to remember that he's got to be cautious, maybe over-cautious. If he makes a mistake it can cost a lot of lives, not just one."

"But he talks like a schoolboy. All that 'knocking the Germans for six' stuff, it makes me sick. He thinks it's a game."

"How d'you get on with the explosives girl?"

"Mary Hamlett?"

"Yes."

"Very well."

"You noticed her hands?"

"They're sort of misshapen you mean?"

"Mary Hamlett's the only SOE girl whom the Germans have caught who got away. But they broke all her fingers on the second day. Every finger and every joint."

"Where was this?"

"Paris, Avenue Foch."

"Why do you tell me this?"

"She's Miles-Hampton's wife, and you can take it from me, he doesn't see the war as a game. He talks like that so that trainees don't get ideas that what they're going to do is glamorous."

She looked at the stolid face. "How old are you, Charles?"

"Twenty-five."

"You remind me of my father."

"How old's he?"

"Fifty something."

"Thanks pal," he said. And she laughed as he started the car.

Fredericks was waiting for them at the cottage.

"They've put forward your drop, it's tonight. Are you both ready?"

They both nodded and Parker said, "You take 'Toinette to get her kit and I'll join you in five minutes."

He felt no regrets at leaving the cottage, or England. He didn't really belong anywhere, the war had come too early in his life for any roots to be disturbed. And he had no fear of either the drop or what might await him at the other end.

• • •

The Dakota was already on the runway as their car pulled up, and they walked with Fredericks to the main hut. There were a few people having drinks at the bar who stared at them as they walked through to one of the rooms at the back. The Field Security sergeant had handed them their clothes in cardboard boxes and had left them to change. Parker turned his back on the girl as he changed his clothes and when Fredericks came in the girl was wearing a thick jersey and a tweed skirt with a coat slung over her arm. Parker wore a well-mended brown woollen suit and a fisherman's heavy jersey.

"Have they checked you both?"

"Yes," said Parker. "They checked us first."

A whole section of SOE spent its time on collecting genuine clothing from countries where agents were dropped. Even innocent travellers to UK ports would lose their luggage and then wonder why they were so generously recompensed. And there was a group of elderly ladies in a basement in Margaret Street who sewed and patched in French, German, Dutch and Belgian styles. They had learned the lessons from experience. German agents were landed in Britain with cloakroom tickets from Berlin nightclubs in their pockets and identity cards that were perfectly forged except that they were machine folded instead of folded by hand.

Their gear was spread along the narrow seat and so were their overalls. They clambered into the thick parachute assemblies. Parker peered out of the door and raised his hand to Fredericks who waved back just as the door was closing.

Inside the aircraft the light was dim and the atmosphere freezing. As they sat side by side on the slatted seat the girl was shaking, and Parker put out his hand to cover hers, their fingers intertwined. The roar of the engines was too loud for them to speak to one another and they had been airborne for more than an hour before they relaxed. Parker stood up and beckoned the girl to stand too. He slowly and carefully checked all the straps on her parachute harness and then checked over the small suitcase that housed her radio and its spares. He dragged out his own two canvas bags from under the seat and checked their fastenings.

Half an hour after they had sat down again the co-pilot had walked back from the cockpit. He bent down to shout in Parker's ear. "The sheet says the girl goes first, is that OK?"

Parker nodded, and the RAF man bent down to shout again.

"You act as despatcher for the girl and I'll do you."

Parker pulled the man's head down to his mouth: "If there's any problem with the girl I shall go out with her."

"You can't do that, sir. It's not allowed."

Parker grinned. "You fix a court of enquiry for when we get back."

The airman rolled his eyes in mock despair and shouted, "About another ten minutes, sir."

There had been a little flak shortly afterwards and Parker guessed that it was probably the defences guarding the German submarine base at Bordeaux. From then on the plane was dropping fast and the co-pilot was standing by the door checking the parachute clips. Then he beckoned them to the white line. Parker attached the girl's cord to the clip and stood behind her as the door swung open. They were at about 4,000 feet and Parker could see a river way below them shining in the moonlight. It must be the Dronne. Then the airman's hand went up and Parker tapped the girl's shoulder. She didn't hesitate for a moment but Parker noticed that her legs were sprawled apart as she fell. He hooked up his own cord and nodded to the airman and jumped.

The cold air was like a steel wall and when the main canopy cracked open he felt no pull because of the numbness of his body. He could see a large white field coming up fast, hit the ground and was rolling, tugging at his chute to spill the air. There was a torch a long way away flashing morse and it flashed a second time and he read: "Bienvenue." He headed for the small dim light, his parachute clutched like a bundle of washing under his arm, his two bags slung across his shoulders. The earth was hard as rock and he stumbled unsteadily in the furrows. They were probably waiting for the frosts to go so that they could harrow and get in some early wheat. Then he dumped the chute and the bags and walked forward slowly and carefully. He was almost in the blackness of the hedge before he realized it was there. And then Devereux's massive frame loomed up. "Welcome back. The girl's OK. I've put her in the hedge."

"Hello, Devereux, I've got to go back for my kit."

"OK. How about I take the 'chute?"

"Yeah, I know, and half the girls in the Corrèze will be wearing white silk knickers."

"No, chief. They dye 'em now. You've been away a long time."

"For Christ's sake what's that. There's a light."

"Ah, that's my surprise."

"What surprise?"

"A car."

"You must be crazy, what about the curfew?"

Devereux laughed softly. "It's the doctor's car, there was a false alarm from a pregnant lady who's overdue."

"You cheeky bastard. How far are we going?"

"Seven, eight kilometres to this side of Brantôme."

"OK, let's get going. Is the doctor in the car?"

"Sure he is."

They picked up the kit and the chutes and stumbled with the girl to the car. The driver was a thin elderly man with a vinegary expression that was relieved only by his blue eyes, and he launched the car into gear the moment they had swung the doors to.

Seven kilometres outside Brantôme they stopped. Parker could see the dim outline of straggling farm buildings.

"Here we are, chief. It's a lousy dump but we daren't go into Brantôme after curfew."

Parker squeezed the doctor's shoulder in thanks, and they all scrambled out. Devereux led them to a wooden building and opened a small door. He whispered. "There's straw and sacks of seed. Let's get settled down. I've got sausage, bread and some brandy."

They piled the bales of straw so that there was an area like a small room. Devereux shone his torch over the girl and then on Parker. "Jesus, you look more tired than when you left. What have they been doing to you?"

"Let me introduce you. 'Toinette, this is Jean-Luc. He's got his own W/T operator but sometimes you may have to take his traffic. Same applies with them as with me. On radio things you're the boss. Nobody, including me, can override you on length of transmissions or timing. They can suggest, but it's your decision." He turned to Devereux, "You understand that, Jean-Luc?"

"OK, chief." He waved a bottle and a package. "Let's have the feast, eh?"

They all slept fitfully until about six o'clock when they washed their faces in the water of a cattle trough. Devereux and Parker had walked across two fields and had burnt the parachutes and buried the metal buckles in a ditch.

It was still pitch black at eight o'clock when they piled into the back of a rusty Fiat van half full of sacks of grain for the mill. There were few people moving in Brantôme as they trundled through and turned on to D939. Twenty minutes later they were on the narrow dirt road up to Puy Henry. Half-way up the steep hill the road stopped and there was just a narrow path to the farm buildings at the top.

Devereux led the way to a cottage that was joined to the main farm building by a stone barn. The old door opened with a massive key. It was a typical Dordogne farm cottage, two up, two down, high ceilings and stone walls at least a metre thick. They opened the shutters and the wintry light barely illumined the white-washed rooms. Parker told the girl to fetch their kit from the van, and as she left he turned to Devereux.

"How secure is this place?"

"You can see anyone approaching for at least ten minutes before they get here, so it's physically well placed. You've rented it for 200 francs a week. The farmer's son was taken by the Germans a year ago to work in Germany. They've not heard from him since, so there's no worry there. They hate the Boche. It's isolated and there's only the one pathway up. There's electricity and a telephone."

Parker nodded, "How many people know I'm here?"

"Me. The farmer and his family, and, I suspect, Frenez and Bonnier know."

"How the hell do they know?"

"I don't know that they do, but there was a rumour from the Commies that you were on your way back."

"Have you been seeing Frenez?"

"Twice. The first time was on instruction from London about an arms drop for Frenez's group. They hadn't had any experience of a big drop. The second time was ten days ago, he came to tell me that they had proof that Grandclement was working with the Germans. He hinted that you were on the way back."

"Is there any food here?"

"Some, not much. Have you got coupons?"

"Sure."

"The farmer can get stuff for you."

Parker moved to the rough kitchen chairs. "Let's talk for a few minutes and then you'd better go. How're things in Brive?"

"We've had orders from London that we still come under you. I've lost Martin and du Champs but we've done a lot of sabotage operations. I expect you saw the radio reports."

"How'd you lose those two?"

"Martin was shot in the chest and neck when we did the power station at Angoulême. We got him away and he had medical treatment but he died about five days later. Du Champs was doing a recce at the telephone exchange at Brive and he was picked up by the police. We did a deal to get him freed but Nolke from the Gestapo at Périgueux happened to visit the jail and he recognized du Champs and he was shipped up to Paris that night."

"To Avenue Foch?"

"Yes. He's in Fresnes now."

"When was this?"

"Last Tuesday."

"And everybody has moved?"

"It's been difficult." Devereux looked embarrassed.

"For God's sake, Jean-Luc, you know the rules—if anybody gets caught—everybody in a reseau gets the hell out of it. You too."

"Nobody's been tailing us, I'm sure of that."

"Devereux, you leave me now, and by midnight I want everybody to have left the district or to have moved their quarters. Bring them into this area if you like, but move them fast."

"OK, chief."

Parker turned to the girl.

"When's your first radio schedule, 'Toinette?"

"It's up to me in the next forty-eight hours. They'll be listening on the hour every hour."

"So."

She looked uncomfortable. "I forgot to change the plug."

His eyes were venomous for a moment. "That was your responsibility, not Beaulieu's," and then he relaxed. "Will it operate with matchsticks and bare wire?"

"I should think so."

"Where is it?"

She pointed to the case amongst the kitbags and she followed him as he walked over. One hand held the wire and the other wrenched off the tell-tale English plug without the benefit of screwdrivers. He walked to the door. "Set it up in the small bedroom for now. We'll find a permanent place tonight. Tell them we've arrived and that we are safe. By the way, what's your security check word?"

She blushed as she looked at him. "I'm not allowed to tell you."

He grinned. "Good girl, but get moving."

He smashed the brown bakelite plug to powder in the yard and dropped the brass terminals through a drain cover. The ground was too hard to dig.

When he had finished he went next door and talked to the farmer and his wife and was satisfied that they wouldn't talk except under real pressure. On the way back he had explored the barn. Except for three calves and a few chickens the place was just storage for hay and straw and a few farm implements. There was a boarded area up near the roof that carried another layer of straw bales and he decided that that was the place for the radio.

• • •

It had been ten o'clock that night before they had put the radio in place, and Parker had laid the aerial along the rafters. As they got back to the cottage Devereux had arrived dishevelled and sweating, despite the cold, from the long walk up the steep hill. Parker stood aggressively, hands on hips, in front of the door. "Are they dispersed?" he asked, almost as if entrance of the cottage would be barred if the answer was unsatisfactory.

"You were right, chief. They've picked up Lachaise. I've dispersed the others."

"Did they get her radio, too?"

"I'm afraid so."

Parker swung round to face the girl. "I'll need to tell London immediately. Can you transmit tonight?"

She nodded. "Yes."

Parker ushered them inside and sat at the kitchen table as he wrote out his message to London, crossing out words as he went to reduce the air-time. He shoved it across to the girl together with his torch.

"Can you manage on your own?"

She nodded, took his pencil, and closed the cottage door behind her as she left.

Parker turned swiftly on Devereux, he spoke through his teeth in anger. "Now you go back to the road, my friend, check whether you've been followed and when you come back come with a plan to rescue Lachaise." He turned away from the other man as if he were no longer there and reached under the table for one of his canvas bags.

He sat there at the table consumed by his anger and frustration, as he looked at the maps. He had come back full of plans for building up the new reseau in the Dordogne, bringing the three reseaux together as an élite force that would harass the Germans over hundreds of square miles. Creating diversions to cover sabotage operations forty or fifty kilometres away. And on his first full day he had to report back that his old reseau from the Corrèze had been dispersed and its highly efficient and experienced girl radio-operator was in the hands of the Gestapo, complete with radio and maybe codes as well. There would be nothing constructive for weeks, just that slow, grinding build-up again. The work of nine months destroyed by the ignoring of elementary security precautions. Devereux had been on the courses and he had been an efficient second-in-command. But as a leader his judgement obviously wasn't good enough. It was a bad start but it was to deal with this kind of situation that they had put him in charge of the three reseaux. He shoved the maps back in his bag and stood up as the girl came in. His eyes checked her for traces of straw or hay but there were none.

"Did you remember to put back the light bulb in the barn?"

The big brown eyes looked at his face. "Don't worry about me, Charles. I shall always stick to the rules. I want to go back alive."

"And the bulb?" he insisted.

"It's back in."

When Devereux came back he was shivering with cold and reported that there had been no watchers and no vehicles and that it was beginning to snow. Parker told him to bed down in the barn.

• • •

Parker had been up at six the next morning, moving round the area of the buildings slowly and cautiously in the dark. Stopping frequently to train his fieldglasses on the pale ribbon of the road to Angoulême and the flickering lights in distant villages. As its name implied, Puy Henry was one of those conical hills that were typical of the area. And as Devereux had said, it was not only isolated, but all the approaches were under observation. There was no dead ground to provide cover for anyone approaching from either the road or the fields below.

He went into the barn and shook Devereux awake.

"Tell me what you know about the Germans in Périgueux."

Devereux shook his head like a dog coming out of water and then dry-washed his face with his hands before he looked with his tired bloodshot eyes at Parker.

"There are two SD men but they cover Angoulême as well. The senior is Heinz Bode and the other is Otto Krugman. There's a Gestapo man who covers this area from Bordeaux."

"What do we know about them?"

"Bode is young, about twenty-six or twenty-seven, a real Nazi lout. Screws anything he can get his hands on. Cunning but not intelligent. Very active. Krugman is about fifty, speaks good French, a ferret, keeps a fantastic card index, moves around the area a lot. Like a country policeman, which he was before the war in Germany. The Gestapo man is Nolke—Gustav Nolke. A professional. Was something senior in the Kriminalpolizei in Germany. He came down here from Paris, he was at the rue de Saussaies and reports direct to them. Then there's hundreds of Feldgendarmerie."

"What are the locals like?"

Devereux shrugged. "About average. Plenty of collaborators; there's a big maquis around Junilac, more around Nontron and Coussac."

"Who oversees them?"

"The Commies. They're spread everywhere, wanting to take over. They want a meeting with you to get more arms. It's a man named Bonnier—Michel Bonnier—the one I mentioned, a very shrewd operator—had training in Moscow before the war."

"And what targets have we got between here and Limoges?"

"Plenty—all the usual stuff— electricity pylons, railway, the big railway workshop in Périgueux, some industry and storage, those big telephone links, God knows how many bridges." Devereux smiled wryly. "There's enough to keep us all happy, chief."

Parker looked at Devereux, aware of the signs of strain on the gaunt face. Devereux was tall and thin, a gangling sort of man, the looks of a gypsy, but brave and loyal. Parker had in mind to send him back to England for more training. But from the hints in London D-day couldn't be more than six or seven months away and he was going to need every good body he could lay hands on.

"What are things like in Limoges?"

"No idea, chief, it's too far away to hear much. They're part of an escape line to Spain that's been very successful and there's a lot of maquis up there."

"You chose this place well, Jean-Luc," and he put his hand on the other man's bent knee. "Let's get something to eat."

• • •

That evening Parker, Devereux and the girl had gone down to Brantôme. They had sat for an hour in the warmth of a small restaurant over bowls of potato soup and a "mique" dumpling, but the presence of groups of German soldiers disturbed the girl so that she could only eat slowly, leaving half her meal untouched. Devereux had pointed out a few of the locals to Parker. The Germans were mainly infantry and signals, but Parker noticed a group of three Waffen SS with the sleeve bands of the 2nd SS Panzer division Das Reich. Most of the Das Reich division were down in the Toulouse area but when D-day came they would be the ones he would have to harass when they were called up to the north to help the German armies repulse any attack on the Channel ports or maybe the Atlantic coast.

It was Parker who had noticed them first because he had automatically taken the seat facing the door. He leaned forward towards the girl and said, "Two Germans have just come in. They're SD. Don't look round. Just go on talking. They'll check our papers, don't panic and go on talking while they look at your papers. If they question you, just charm them. Listen to me and let me give my papers up first." Parker would have recognized the two SD men even without Devereux's description.

The tall one, Bode, was the standard Nazi, fair wavy hair, blue eyes, and he stood with both hands stuck in his leather belt while Krugman carefully checked the papers. Bode looked at the people at the various tables as he leaned against the closed door. The *patron* moved among his customers trying to make things seem normal. Even the German soldiers had fallen silent.

Both Parker and Devereux had put their papers on the table and had gone on eating. Krugman came to their table last and Parker handed up his identity card and his German pass that allowed him to move between what had been the Occupied Zone and the Unoccupied Zone until the Germans had broken their treaty with Vichy and occupied the whole of France.

Krugman was whistling softly to himself as he looked at the identity card.

"Your name?"

"Chaland—Charles."

"When were you born?"

"7 December 1916."

"Where?"

"Madagascar—Diego Suarez."

"Occupation?"

"Agricultural engineer."

Krugman put down the identity card and examined the German pass. He waved it idly in front of Parker's face.

"Why do you need this?"

Parker laughed. "Tractors break down, my friend, both sides of the zone borders."

"So?"

"So what?"

"Why does it need to be you who fixes them?"

"Ask your people in Paris, my friend. They decide these things not me."

Krugman was tapping the pass against his chin as he looked at Parker.

"What was the name of the German officer who signed your pass?"

"I've no idea. I'm a Frenchman. I don't read German script."

Krugman nodded and then put down the pass on the table and went through the same ritual with Devereux. When he came to the girl Bode walked over from the door, looking over the girl with a supercilious smile. He stood while Krugman checked her card and watched her as Krugman put his questions.

"Name?"

"Cousteau—Antoinette."

"Born?"

"3 August 1920."

"Place of birth?"

"Seychelles—Mahé."

Bode smiled at his colleague: "Looks like we've got the Foreign Legion here, Otto."

He turned to the girl. "And what are you doing here?"

"I'm with Monsieur Chaland. I am his assistant."

"What's your occupation?"

"I'm a botanist. I deal with pests."

There was a laugh from one of the soldiers who obviously understood French, and Bode turned round slowly to look at the men in the green uniforms. They were still smiling and the provocation was too much. He walked over to their table and asked for their documents and Krugman joined him. Five minutes later they had left.

Parker poured another drink for them all.

"Don't get up, 'Toinette. They'll wait outside to see who goes first. We'll go when the others go. You did well, girl. If you stand up to the bastards they generally back down if they aren't really suspicious."

They walked back to the cottage at Puy Henry and sat talking. The farmer had put a heap of logs outside the cottage door and a bowl with four eggs laid in straw.

All the next day Parker had called on local farmers offering his services and he had been welcomed, and given enough offers of work to last him for months. At one of the biggest estates he had been taken to see the owner, the Comte de Mansard, a tall patrician Frenchman whose shrewd eyes had watched him intently as Parker answered his questions. Finally, he had put on his coat and walked with Parker across the frozen grass of the wide lawns. When they were well clear of the manor house the man had stopped.

"Nobody can hear us now, Monsieur Chaland. But you speak very good French for an Englishman."

Parker returned the man's stare without speaking, and the man continued. "I've got a brother in Dachau, monsieur, and I'm watched constantly by the Germans. My younger sister is in London working for de Gaulle. It is almost impossible for me to help you openly but I can tell you a lot about people in this area. You could use me as a reference point when you have doubts. My family have been here for centuries. We know everybody in the area and we still have influence if you need it. There is only my wife and myself here, and a few servants who have been with us since my father's days."

"Who are the people you think could help me?"

"Let me say that very few will not help you. It would be easier for me to tell you the collaborators."

"Who are they?"

"The mayor licks the Germans' boots, the man who owns the engineering factory at Mareuil is making a fortune from the Germans. Two senior policemen are strong Pétainists. There are others whom I would not trust but you make your own judgments first."

"What about your farm-workers?"

"All Frenchmen, true Frenchmen."

"Could we have meetings here, eight or nine people?"

The man shrugged and smiled. "My home is yours, Monsieur Chaland. My wife and I have nothing to lose but our lives."

Parker held out his hand and the man took it and held it. "How long will it be, monsieur? How long?"

"Not long, monsieur. But it will seem long, there is so much to be done." And he walked away to the lodge where he had left his cycle. It started to snow as he got to the main road.

That morning when he was in Périgueux he had rented a room and paid six months' rent in advance. It was in one of the small streets between the cathedral and the river, and the most desirable feature of the house was that it had separate entrances back and forth. He said nothing to the girl or Devereux about the room, or the radio he had left in the dusty attic.

They were eating their evening meal when there was a knock on the door. It was a gentle knock but loud enough for them to make out the morse V-sign. Parker had gone to the door still chewing, and when he opened the door he saw a girl; there were snowflakes on her eye-lashes and around the edge of the hood she wore. She said, "I bring a message from Michel to Monsieur Chaland."

He stood back from the door and signalled to her to step inside. He saw her eyes take in the room and the others at the table. "Would you like some coffee, have you eaten?"

She shook her head: "Maybe just some warm water."

Parker nodded to 'Toinette. "Get her some coffee and cheese with bread." Then he turned to the girl: "We'll go upstairs."

She followed him up to the bedroom. With reflexed caution he went to 'Toinette's room, not his own. He waved the girl to the low bed and sat on a box facing her. "Take off your coat while you talk."

She was so dark-skinned that she could be Greek, and her big eyes were almost black with no discernible difference of colour between the pupils and the dark irises. Her mouth was full and sensuous but she had no air of sexuality and her face had only the beauty of calmness. She was not pretty but certainly not plain. She was attractive as a child or a timid animal is attractive. She leaned forward as she pushed aside her coat and hood and he noticed that she made no feminine gesture to arrange her hair.

"What was the message from Michel?"

"He would like to meet you and wishes to co-operate with your organization."

"What is your name, mam'selle?"

"Sabine."

"And where does Michel suggest that we meet?"

"He will attend wherever you wish."

"Can I see your identity card?"

She reached for the pocket of her coat and pulled out an old leather wallet that was held together with a broad elastic band. She pulled out the card and handed it to him, and he looked at it carefully. The photographs matched and he checked the details. "Nom: Patou. Prénoms: Sabine. Né. le 3 Janvier 1925. Sexe: F. Français par: Filiation. Situation de Famille: Fille non mariée. Occupation: Maitresse décole." The physical description was accurate and the card was valid until 28.12.53. The Germans were looking that far ahead for the Thousand Year Reich.

Parker looked across at her as he handed back the card. She had sat there humbly and patiently as he checked her credentials and for a moment he found the humility touching and sad.

"Tell Michel that I will meet him one week from today at

the museum in Périgueux at eleven. Tell him to be looking at the Sèvres porcelain. The password will be 'Champs Elysées.' Then we walk outside separately and cross the road to the park."

She stood up, reaching for her coat.

"You can stay here for the night or you'll be caught in the curfew."

Chapter Four

For five days he had circulated through the area, interviewing volunteers and checking one against the other. He had set Devereux to gather together two or three of his displaced circuit to check the layout and procedure at the jail. He had had several conferences with the Comte de Mansard at the manor house and had crossed off the names of two volunteers from his list. He had welded new tines on to a cultivator and stripped down, cleaned and re-assembled a disc-harrow. He was sure that both farmers knew that he was to do with the Resistance. Both had offered him payment in off-the-ration meat and vegetables, and he had accepted gladly but had made out an invoice in francs and given a receipt.

• • •

The only person looking at the Sèvres exhibits was a man. Aged about thirty with dark curly hair, a broken nose set in a round fat face, barrel-chested and wearing workmen's overalls. He had turned as Parker stood alongside him and without any pause he had said, "Les Champs Elysées sont pour les Boches aujourd'hui." And he grinned as he held out his hand. Parker took it briefly then turned and walked away.

They had sat on a bench while young mothers wheeled tattered prams along the paths, and children played with hoops and blew on cold fingers before tucking them under their arms.

"Your courier told me you needed help."

"Then she misinformed you, Chaland. I said we could co-operate, that is all."

"What kind of co-operation?"

"We need things that you can supply and we will help you in any way you ask."

Parker looked at the round, brown face. "You mean if your masters in Moscow say that you can."

The grey eyes and the thin mouth showed their anger. "We take orders from nobody. I give the orders."

"You people were co-operating happily with the Germans until they invaded Russia. The Party line could change again next week."

"I never co-operated with the Germans at any time. I came down here from Paris the day Pétain took over. I've never been back."

"What is it you need?"

"Arms and ammunition. Rifles, machine-guns, mortars, grenades, flares and medical supplies."

Parker stood up. "Let's walk, we'll look odd sitting here in the freezing cold. Have you got anywhere safer in this place?"

"They'll give us a room at Chez Victor."

• • •

They had sat in the unlit room with a bottle of wine and some cheese. There was no bread that day.

"How did you know where I was, Michel?"

"I heard talk from two of Devereux's men that you were coming back. They weren't so bright you know after you had gone, but I hear you've pulled them out and they're in this area now."

"Who were the talkers?"

"The one the Germans picked up, I've forgotten his name, and the other was the kid from the telephone exchange, André."

"André Bourdeille?"

"That's the one."

"Why did he talk?"

Bonnier grinned. "The usual reason; wanted to impress a girl he was trying to screw, one of mine." He laughed as he looked at Parker's disgust. "He never made it, Chaland, but he was trying hard."

"How many men have you got?"

Bonnier's grey eyes were on Parker's face, working something out. "Are you on my side, Chaland?"

"I'm on the side of anyone who'll fight the Germans."

"I've got over two thousand maquis but very few arms."

Parker pushed the wine bottle to one side and leaned forward on the table, looking at Bonnier.

"And if you get the arms you'll go rampaging around the countryside shooting the Boche and they'll take civilian reprisals."

"What would you have us do?" And the anger was no longer concealed.

Parker brushed up some crumbs of cheese and put them in his mouth. "You could train with your arms, you could plan ambushes and tactics and be ready to operate when it really mattered."

Bonnier's eyes half closed: "Are your people really going to come?"

"They're going to come all right."

"When?"

Parker smiled. "If I knew I couldn't tell you. But I haven't come back here for a quiet life, Bonnier. I'm an Englishman remember, not a Frenchman."

Bonnier smiled. "When it's all over and I'm mayor of Périgueux we'll make you a Frenchman."

"Maybe we'll do that, Michel."

Bonnier noted the Christian name, and Parker noted what he had always suspected; that when it was all over the Communists expected to be running the country.

"If I get you a first drop of supplies it will be on three conditions. First, that you accept a British officer, an arms expert from London, to train your people. Second, that you control your people until we give you the word. A few small jobs maybe, but you don't start stirring up the Germans until we're ready. And third, that the drop is organized by me together with you. Even a token drop will take three aircraft. We've got the experience, you haven't."

Bonnier shrugged. "Beggars can't be choosers, Chaland."

"That's not good enough, my friend. Beggars can make a bloody nuisance of themselves once they've got the material. This is going to be one part of France where we all work together. No politics, no post-war vote catching, no bloody heroes."

Bonnier put his hand out palm upwards on the table. "Agreed, my friend. In writing if you wish. My men's morale will go sky-high with supplies; they'll do what I say."

As Parker put his hand on Bonnier's open hand, Bonnier's eyes glistened with tears: "Will they come, Charles, will it ever come right again?"

"They'll come. It won't be long. And it will be all over for all of us."

"We Frenchmen will remember, Chaland. You'll see."

Parker smiled and although his words were harsh his smile was friendly. "When it's all over, my friend, de Gaulle will see that you don't remember, not the Englishmen anyway. And you'll find that all the world will claim to have been in the Resistance then. You won't find a collaborator in all France."

Bonnier was silent as he absorbed what Parker had said. He had obviously never seriously considered what the real end of the German occupation might mean. As Parker went to stand up Bonnier looked up at him.

"Do you want help to get your radio girl out of jail?"

"You mean Lachaise?"

"Sure."

"I need a van or an ambulance and a taxi."

"I'll fix both. When do you want them?"

"Can you send your courier girl early tomorrow morning

and I'll give her the details. It's going to be in the next forty-eight hours."

"You know she's in a bad way?"

"No. How bad?"

"I've got contacts in there. She hasn't talked and they've burnt her feet and her hands. They've refused her any medical help. She won't live too long."

"Who did it?"

"Nolke."

"Could you fix the transport by this afternoon?"

Bonnier stood up and said softly, "Leave it to me."

• • •

The van, an ambulance and the taxi were parked at the end of the road up the hill to the cottage at Puy Henry by the time Parker had cycled back. There was a message for him with 'Toinette.

"Michel Bonnier came with the vehicles and he's waiting with his men down in the bottom field. There's a sheep shed there. He wants to see you urgently. If you'll flash him a 'V' on your torch he'll come up."

Parker had walked away from the cottage and flashed his torch into the darkness. He flashed just once, and despite the cold he stood waiting. It was nearly twenty minutes before he saw Bonnier's breath as he came up the last few metres.

"Let's go inside. How are your men down there?"

"OK, Chaland. You saw the ambulance?"

"Yes."

"I hear that they're taking Lachaise to a doctor at Brive early tomorrow morning. He's a physician who does a lot for the Germans on the side. Abortions, magic VD cures and the like."

"Any idea what they're going to get him to do?"

"No idea. Death certificate, make her fit enough to send to Paris. God knows."

They were inside the cottage and Parker saw Bonnier's eyes take in the layout. He introduced 'Toinette without explanation and Devereux nodded a silent acknowledgement. Parker waved Bonnier to a chair at the table and spread out the town map. He looked up at Bonnier.

"We'll have to get the vehicles and men in place before the curfew tonight. I'm thinking of an ambush."

"There's a double junction at Thenon. We could have men both sides of the main road. The taxi can come out from the south road to block their ambulance. We'll take out the girl and transfer her to our ambulance and we could have her in Toulouse before the day's out."

Parker looked at his watch. "We've got just over two hours before curfew. How many of your men are with you?"

"Five, and Sabine."

"Will you get the ambulance down to Thenon?" Parker looked across at Devereux. "Where can we leave it near the cross-roads?"

Devereux shrugged. "At Doisneau's barn or in the yard at the mill."

"You go with Bonnier, Jean-Luc, and I'll meet you by the post office at Thenon at . . ." He looked at his watch ". . . at eight-twenty."

Parker looked back at Bonnier. "What weapons have you got with you?"

"Two Lugers, a Lee-Enfield ·303 and a submachine-gun."

"What's the machine-gun?"

"German. A Schmeisser."

"D'you want to leave Sabine here? 'Toinette will be staying here."

"No. Better she stays with my people."

"Have you got any medical connections in Toulouse?"

Bonnier grimaced and shrugged. "We have no connections anywhere, my friend. Only you people have connections."

Parker stood up. "I'll see you there, Michel. Thanks for the vehicles. Where did they come from?"

Bonnier stood up slowly, slightly resenting the question. "The van is from the priest at Agonac, the ambulance we have had for two months and the taxi was stolen from Bordeaux a year ago. We've changed all the numbers for tonight."

'Toinette was leaning against the wall and after Parker had closed the door he said: "Send a signal to Baker Street. We want medical help near Toulouse or even Perpignan by tomorrow afternoon. Tell them that it will be fractures, burns and the usual Gestapo stuff. Tell them what we're doing. Mention Bonnier's help. And make it short. When you've sent the signal close the cottage but don't lock the door, and stay in the barn. Up the top where the radio is. Don't come down until you hear me. I'll whistle something. What d'you fancy?"

'Toinette smiled. "Let's have 'Vous qui passez sans me voir.'"

For only the second time since she had known him Parker almost smiled. He pulled the cottage door to behind him as he left.

He cycled to the lodge then walked his cycle up the drive to the manor house and rested it against the steps. There were no lights showing and the bell echoed emptily long after he had pulled it. Minutes later the door had opened slightly. An old man looked at him with watery eyes, then recognizing him, he opened the door for Parker to go in. The old man led the way to a room at the back of the house. There was no knocking on doors; the old man fumbled and then pushed open the door.

A woman sat sewing, and the count himself was bending to put a log on the small fire burning in the massive fireplace. He stood up, recognized Parker and came to greet him.

"My wife, Monsieur Chaland." The woman looked up from her sewing and nodded to Parker. "It is quite safe to talk. Is there trouble?"

"I need a doctor, Monsieur le Comte."

The count's pale blue eyes wandered over Parker's face as he tried to work out why a doctor should be needed by the Resistance and then either gave up the attempt or guessed an answer.

"There's old Pignon in the village. He'd be very safe. Or there's Renard in Périgueux."

Parker looked at the man's face. "It's for serious burns and probably broken bones. A girl."

The count spoke very softly. "The girl in jail in Périgueux?"

Parker nodded.

"It's old Pignon then. I'll phone him. How long has he got?"

Parker shrugged. "I want him as soon as possible. But he doesn't *have* to come. It's voluntary."

The count shook his head. "It's not. But he'll love it."

He spoke briefly on the telephone and then walked back to Parker. "He's on his way." He waved Parker to a big chair and sat opposite holding one hand to the small flames of the fire. "He's a drunk. He used to be a leading physician in Paris. He came down here when the Germans took Paris. He'll help you any way you need. But he's over seventy."

The count stood up. "A drink, Chaland?"

"I don't drink, Monsieur le Comte."

"A brandy perhaps, against the cold."

"Brandy's for pain."

The tall elderly man poured himself a glass of wine from a decanter and with the glass to his lips he looked at the man sitting uncomfortably in the comfortable chair. The face was quite ordinary, not particularly English, nor typically French. The brown eyes were a little light, the brown hair nondescript, the skin tanned by an outdoor life, not on the Riviera. The mouth was full and firm and there were muscles at the jaws. But there was an air of total confidence about the man. He would ask for the impossible and he would get it and not be surprised. No social graces, no charm, but an air of integrity that would appeal to a woman. He could imagine men following this man blindly. He wondered what possessed an Englishman to fight the Germans in France rather than with his compatriots. A strange people the English. Did the Romans and the Normans go too far, or not far enough.

The door opened to cut short his thoughts. It was the doctor, his face glowing pink from the cold, the broken capillaries on his cheeks could easily be mistaken for the glow of good health rather than excessive drink.

"Pignon, let me introduce Monsieur Chaland. Our mutual friend in need."

The old doctor closed one eye to peer at Parker as he held out his hand. "Good evening, my friend, tell me what I can do."

Parker took in the bent figure of the old man and noticed

the swollen knuckle joints on the hand that clasped the black medical bag.

"It means spending the night under bad conditions. No food, no heating. Then travelling in an ambulance to somewhere near Toulouse. Giving medical treatment to a girl who is at least badly burnt, probably a number of small broken bones. A fair chance of being caught by the Germans and the girl is a Gestapo prisoner."

The bent figure shifted only slightly. "I am at your disposal, Monsieur Chaland."

Parker looked at the count. "Could the doctor and I be driven to Puy Henry? It's a question of time."

"There's a lorry already loaded with vegetables to go to Périgueux, we could use that."

The doctor had sat alongside the count as he drove the ancient lorry, and Parker lay on the hard sacks of potatoes with his bicycle.

Parker waved the old man to the taxi and shouted his thanks to the count. He found the ignition keys in the taxi and the "Fahrschein" on the seat. He glanced at the photograph on the identity card. It was nothing like him but it would have to do. If he were caught by the Germans or the police without a "Fahrschein" he would be arrested instantly.

He drove through the back streets of Périgueux, and as they got to the N89 to Brive there was steam coming from the radiator cap. They stopped just outside the town at an isolated cottage and Parker begged a gallon of water and poured it in with the engine still running.

They were five minutes late at Thenon and there were only twenty minutes left before curfew. He parked the taxi at the back of the cemetery and hurried to the post office. Devereux saw him coming and went towards him. "We've found a better place at la Garde. There's a scrapyard with big double gates. Bonnier's already got the keys and they're in there waiting for you."

When Parker had seen the scrapyard he walked back to the main road. He walked slowly in the dark, pacing out the widths of the converging minor roads to the north and south. When he got back there were Bonnier's men guarding the doors and Bonnier himself was in the ambulance lying on the leather bed. He sat up as Parker stepped in through the rear door.

I've taken a room at the road-mender's cottage and his old woman's cooking the stuff I bought."

"Have you got your own maps?"

"Some."

"Let's go and eat then."

• • •

After the meal had been cleared away they spread the maps across the table. Parker pushed his finger at the map. "We'll ambush them here at la Garde. It's about three kilometres short of Thenon. There're no telephones, no police." He looked up at Bonnier. "I've got a feeling they'll have an escort of some kind. Are you prepared to take them on?"

Bonnier grinned. "You give the orders and we'll carry them out."

"The doctor will stay in the ambulance with your girl. How many torches have we got?"

"We've got four."

"I've got one. There's a bend in the road. Put one of your men at the start of the bend and he signals just after they pass. The taxi is waiting and he starts the engine at the signal. The engine's got to be warm. He'll get about two minutes to start the engine and move across on to the road. Say fifty metres. The taxi must make actual impact with the ambulance or the escort. Your look-out has the machine-gun and he covers the road behind so they can't back away the rear vehicle if there are two. Tires first, then escort. We don't want any survivors. You and I can deal with them. Two of your men in the ditch, one each side of the main road. The road's not wide enough for them to turn a vehicle on one lock. When we've dealt with the Germans you send a runner back to bring up our ambulance and we transfer the girl."

Parker nodded and looked at Devereux. "You know these parts, Devereux. Are there any houses up the little road on the north side?"

"A row of cottages on the left-hand side. Three or four then nothing until Ajat."

"How far's that?"

"Two, maybe three, kilometres."

"And after Ajat?"

"Virtually nothing until Brouchaud. Say ten kilometres."

"OK." He turned to Bonnier. "Michel, when the ambulance has gone, remove their vehicles, whatever they are, to halfway between Brouchaud and Ajat. Smash the cylinder heads and pistons if you've got time." He turned to Devereux. "Jean-Luc, you'll drive the girl down to Toulouse. I'll give you an address in Toulouse. And in case it doesn't work I'll give you another address, in Perpignan. When there's any news you phone Monsieur le Comte—I'll give you his number. Leave a brief message for me—two words or three. Depending on what you find you'll leave the girl and make your own way back to Puy Henry. Understood?"

Devereux went on picking his teeth as he nodded. Parker looked back at Bonnier. "We'll have to dump your taxi as well. A pity."

Bonnier shrugged. "I'll take my men off as soon as we've cleared the vehicles." The blue eyes looked at Parker's face. "Do we get our arms drop then?"

"You'd have got it without this, Michel. You go and give your men their instructions. Tell them to expect the Germans any time after eleven."

• • •

Parker and Bonnier had walked together to the corner of the main road. As they stood there Parker realized that he had made what could be a fatal error. "Michel, send one of your boys up to the look-out who is going to signal us. Tell him to give us a test flash now. A 'V' in morse will do."

Parker had stood straining his eyes into the darkness for five minutes and then he saw the flashes and he shone his own torch back to give the sentry a guide to the right line of sight.

Bonnier rejoined Parker. "Is that OK, Chaland?"

"That's fine—shall I check your weapon?" Bonnier handed

over his gun and Parker turned it to take advantage of the faint light of the moon. He bent his head to check the trigger guard.

"D'you realize what this is, Michel?"

"One of my fellows said it was a Schmeisser machine-gun."

Parker looked at Bonnier in disbelief. "That means you've never fired it?"

"There's only thirty rounds."

Parker handed over his Luger. "This is the thumb safety catch. Up, for the firing position. You can have your weapon back afterwards. You'd better watch what I'm doing but we'll have to face that way to make sure we see the signal." Parker pointed. "This is the lock pin and it's not properly home, which means that the whole trigger mechanism would swing down if you fired it. This isn't a machine-gun, it's an assault rifle, and it's very modern. I won't ask where you got it, but it's only been German Army issue for about nine months. It's called an StG44. This trap slides back and this is the magazine filler. Let's get the chamber off."

Parker had eased out the badly loaded cartridges and reloaded the chamber and snapped it back into the housing. He looked up at Bonnier: "I'll show you how to use this thing next week."

They both faced the direction of the bend in the road and at the corner of the road they heard the taxi's engine churn and then catch. It was switched off quickly and then started again. The second time it caught immediately. It was only twenty metres away but it was quite invisible.

The two men leaned on the low stone wall over a culvert. They were silent for several minutes and then Bonnier said, "Have you contacted your people about a drop for me?"

"Yes."

"Any reply?"

"Not yet, but the reply will only concern what and where. Have you got any suitable places in mind?"

"My base is at Bournaud and there are big areas under our control there—look, my God, there's the torch."

They both ran to the cross-roads and Parker banged on the side of the taxi as he ran. It started easily and rolled past them to the edge of the main road. And then they saw the headlights of two army motorcyclists. He shouted to Bonnier, "Let them pass."

He ran to the taxi and shouted, "Wait for the ambulance. Hit it right on the nose." And then they could see the lights of the ambulance, even its white paint. He was conscious of the taxi lurching forward into the main road. It hit the ambulance and he saw the radiators smash together and the ambulance slewed sideways across the road, and then there was a burst of firing and single shots. There was another pair of motorcyclists covering the rear of the ambulance, and as Parker wrenched open the driving door of the ambulance he was conscious of a motorcycle headlight from a bike lying on its side on the road, and then a shower of orange sparks as the second bike ground along on its side, its foot-pedal gouging up the road surface.

As the door swung open Parker reached up and grabbed the driver's collar. The man held on to the wheel as Parker wrenched at him but slowly his grip gave and he was dragged to the road. Parker hit him behind the ear with the StG44 and raced to the rear doors. They were not locked and he pulled down the mobile steps and jumped in. There was no light inside the ambulance. He shone his torch on the figure strapped to the leather bed. There were two thin grey hospital blankets over the girl, covering half her face as well as her body. He pulled back the blankets and shone the torch on her face. He thought at first that she was dead but there was a nerve fibrillating in her cheek. Her face was a waxy yellow with yellow bruises along her jaw and small circular burns from cigarettes on both her cheeks. He slowly pulled the blankets from her body. She was naked and as he moved the torch along her body he trembled with anger. One breast was a suppurating mass and there were electrode burns on her stomach and pelvis. For a moment he closed his eyes tight and held his head as if he were praying. But he wasn't.

Then the ambulance swayed as someone climbed aboard. He turned his torch on. It was Bonnier, grinning in triumph. "All four cyclists finished. We stripped them. Fantastic. Uniforms and documents and the bikes. Four almost new

BMWs." Then he saw Parker's face. "Christ, how's the girl?"

"She must be almost finished. Get our ambulance and the doctor. And tell Devereux to get a shift on. I'll stay here."

Devereux, the doctor and Sabine were there in less than three minutes. The doctor bent over the girl, his hand holding her wrist, and he pulled back the lid of one eye as Parker shone his torch on the girl. He could see the doctor's lips silently counting and then he stood up and looked at Parker. "If God cares I can keep her alive for about thirty-six hours, but no longer. She needs hospital care, and drugs I could never get."

"And if God doesn't care?"

A voice, a girl's voice, said softly, "He does care."

Parker moved the torch and saw Sabine kneeling alongside the girl, her arm cradling the girl's head, and he said harshly, "You'll make her worse doing that." He looked at the doctor for confirmation but Pignon shrugged. "It will make no difference, monsieur. Time, however, will make a difference."

They had carefully transferred the dying girl to the other ambulance and Devereux had driven off into the night. The doctor had said that he thought he could bluff his way through any normal curfew checks.

Parker stood at the side of the road. He realized that he had said no word of praise or thanks to the doctor.

While Bonnier's men towed away the damaged ambulance and the taxi Parker stood watching for oncoming vehicles. He shone his torch to look at his watch. It was only one-thirty. Bonnier came back to him. "What are you going to do, Chaland?"

"I'll have to stay here tonight."

"Can you look after Sabine? I can't take her with the motorcycles."

"Yes. Send her back to the scrapyard and tell her to wait for me. Would the road-mender put us up d'you think?"

Bonnier shook his head. "Not after this lot. He'll be frightened silly."

Parker had heard the motorcycles head off up the side-road and then he was alone. Everywhere was silent, and despite the cold he could feel trickles of sweat running down his back. The sky was clear now, and he could see a few stars. And in the stillness and the silence he wondered if he were mad. Victoria Road, Aston, seemed incredibly far away. He shivered and then set off for the scrapyard.

The girl was huddled against a pile of rusty cylinder blocks.

He found a piece of tarpaulin and made a roof over their heads. He sat close to the girl and a line of pale moonlight washed her face. She turned to look at him.

"Are the Germans all right?"

"Which Germans?"

"Those on the motorcycles."

Parker looked to see if she were smiling. She wasn't. "They're fine, Sabine. Dead as pigs."

"Were they old or young?"

"I've no idea."

"You don't mind that they're dead."

"I'm glad that they're dead."

"But they're men. Fathers, husbands, sons."

"Sons of bitches."

"There are people who love them, who think they are still alive."

"How old are you, Sabine?"

"Eighteen."

"Where were you when the Germans smashed France?"

"In Paris."

"Well, out on the country roads there were tens of thousands of old people, and women and children, and those bastard Germans machine-gunned them down. Not just to kill them mind you, but to block the roads so that the French army couldn't get away. Those refugees were loved by people too." He turned towards her almost violently, his fist slamming into his open palm. "Those pigs started it all. They kill people like they are animals, in gas chambers and Christ knows what. They smash their way round France as if we were scum."

The girl put her head on one side to see him more clearly, and she said softly, "But you're not French."

"Who says so?"

"Your words. You speak very fluently but you use old-fashioned words that my mother uses."

He looked at her face. "Where is your mother?"

"She's dead. She was one of the refugees they killed outside Lyons. The Messerschmitts."

"What happened to you?"

"Some soldiers gave me a lift in a truck."

"Where did you go to?"

"Not far."

And there was something in her voice that made him look at her face. And as if he had asked a question she said, "They raped me and threw me out into a ditch."

"And now you feel soft for Germans, girl?"

"They were French soldiers, Monsieur Chaland."

He closed his eyes. "God Almighty, what a world."

"And what about you. Your mother, your father?"

"My father died years ago. My mother's still alive; she lives in a dream world where my father's still alive."

"And why do you risk your life here in France?"

It was a long time before he answered. "When I was a small boy my mother talked all the time about France. She was French. Everything that was good was French. The songs, the people, the artists, the countryside. I grew up to believe that the skies were bluer in France, the marigolds more golden, and the people all poets or artists or farmers. I'd been to France many times. I must have seen it wasn't true. But I looked without seeing and that's how France has always been for me. I know now that it isn't true, but that makes no difference. This country is where the world begins for me. I love it without liking it. And *that's* why I'm here."

She leaned back against the rusty metal blocks and patted her shoulder. "Put your head on my shoulder and sleep. You must be very tired."

She could see either confusion or indignation on his face that she should think he needed any such comfort. She smiled and put her arm through his. "Let's both sleep."

Chapter Five

During the next two weeks he had crossed and re-crossed a dozen times the vast triangle of his territory. At Limoges he had found Frenez and his reseau with a dozen operations waiting for his approval but with a desperate need for a radio operator and explosives.

There had been a three-plane drop for Bonnier's maquisards and a Lysander operation bringing a three-man team to train Bonnier's men.

He had given Devereux command of the Périgueux reseau despite his shortcomings. But only after he had recruited Lemaire, who ran the garage at the edge of the town. Lemaire was a solid type from Paris who had set up the garage in 1938 and was now part of the Périgord.

They had found a lodging for 'Toinette near the garage, and her radio was housed in the side-wall of the deep servicing pit in the workshop and she used an abandoned storeroom for her transmissions. When she was transmitting, Lemaire and his men kept an eye out for the Germans.

In the last week in February the three reseaux had been given a trial run on a joint operation. They had blown railway tracks at Uzerche and La Rochefoucauld, a power line at Nontron, and had completely destroyed the telephone exchange at Dignac. There had been thirty-two men in the groups and the only casualty was a burnt foot at the pylon, and that was from a timing device wrongly set.

Parker sat eating bread and cheese in the cottage at Puy Henry as the rain lashed down outside. The local newspaper was spread across the kitchen table so that he could read as he ate. He was wiping his hand across his mouth as he saw the item. A local bank had been robbed of 150,000 francs. Hooligans with guns had held up the manager and his staff, and had fired shots into the ceiling. They had left on motorcycles and it stank of Bonnier's men. As he folded the paper he heard the sound of a car. Then silence. He pulled out his pad of work tickets and invoices and waited for the knock.

It was 'Toinette. Lemaire had stayed with the car. She pulled out several sheets of message pad. He took them from her and handed her a three-page message for encoding. "Don't wait, 'Toinette. I'll bring my stuff down to you this evening."

He bent down to read the messages on the table and he was aware that the girl was still there. There were three messages:

18 4 9 7 12 3 1 8
YOUR /709/A
CKNOW LED
GED/RA F/BO
MBED/T RAN
SPORT ERS/
ESTIM ATE
D/SIXO/ THO
THOUS AND
GALLO NS/D
ESTRO YED/
CONGR ATU
LATIO NS/S
204

The second was the map references for a Lysander operation to bring over an additional radio operator.

The third message expressed regret at informing him of his mother's death from pneumonia. Did he have instructions on a burial place.

He sat at the table and wrote out his replies and several more requests and reports to London. He looked up at 'Toinette. She was leaning forward, her eyes on his face, and he was suddenly aware of her breasts. He was tempted to put out a hand and touch them. But it was only a fleeting image. It would mean an obligation. He'd got too many of those.

"I've put them in order of urgency, 'Toinette. How are things down at the garage?"

"I was sad about your mother, Charles."

He stood up. "Be sad for those who are still alive. How are things at the garage?"

"The Germans came yesterday. They found nothing and I wasn't there. They questioned Lemaire about the vehicles in the garage."

She stood with his messages in her hand as if she wanted to say something.

"What is it 'Toinette?"

She smiled. "You don't miss a thing, do you. Is it all right if I move my place?"

"Who is he?"

She laughed. "How the hell did you know?"

"Who is he?"

"It's Victor, the schoolmaster."

Victor had been in the French army. He was a member of the reseau and lived in a small apartment in Périgueux. Parker looked intently at the girl. "Have you been sleeping with him?"

"Yes."

"At your place?"

"Yes."

"Why don't you leave it at that?"

"I could look after him. We'd like to be together."

"You remember what they told you at Wanborough Manor—no emotional involvements."

"I'd be OK, Charles. Really."

He shook his head: "If you move to Victor's place I'll have to send you back to England. You'd be a danger."

"But why? Why only me? Everybody in the reseau sleeps with somebody."

"It would be safer if they didn't. But sleeping is one thing, an emotional relationship is something else. If Victor is picked up it's a pressure point on you. Or it could be the other way round. You both need to be single-minded for this work. It's not just *your* lives, it's everybody in the group. But you heard all this while you were training."

He could see the anger and frustration on her face. "Don't you ever think of anything except this bloody game? Every girl in the reseau would hoist her skirt up for *you* but you wouldn't bloody well notice if they did."

He smiled. "That's why Baker Street sends me all the pretty girls. It won't be long 'Toinette, and then it'll all be over."

She looked at his face, shaking her head in mystification, but she was half smiling.

• • •

He had cycled down to Périgueux and left his cycle at the garage and then walked to his room on the other side of the town. It was just as he had left it, neat and tidy, quiet and calm. He reached under the small table, eased out the two drawing pins, and the small block of paper had come away. It was a one-time code pad and he sat for over an hour encoding his report to London. When he had finished he pinned the unused sheets of the pad back in place, and stood looking out of the window as the light faded.

There seemed to be more Germans in the town than a week ago, and more military vehicles. The influx of refugees from Alsace had doubled the population. Shopkeepers were putting up the shutters for the night and the café opposite was quite full. And then in the light from the *pâtisserie* he saw Sabine, and a few metres behind her was the Gestapo man Nolke. In a few strides he had caught up with the girl and she stood still as he spoke to her. She shook her head and walked on but Nolke caught her shoulder and spun her round to face him. The German's head was nodding as if to emphasize his words and the girl's face was just a faint blur. Parker looked at his watch. He had an hour before his transmission schedule came up. He locked the door behind him and raced down the stairs. Across the road he could see Nolke and the girl, his hand gripping the girl's arm. Nolke was not in uniform, he was wearing a black leather coat and a beret. When Parker got up to them he stopped.

He looked at Sabine. "Hello, darling," and he turned to look at Nolke, puzzled but amiable. "I don't think I know you, monsieur."

Nolke's eyes went over Parker's face. "Your papers."

"Who the hell are you to ask for my papers?"

"Gestapo, my friend. Let's have your papers."

Parker kept his eyes away from the girl. "I've never heard of Gestapo people in Périgueux. Let's go to the police station." And he slid his arm into the girl's and stood waiting, looking at Nolke, who hesitated and then stepped into the road and waved down an army lorry. When the driver stopped and put his head out Nolke said, "Ich hab' ein Gefangener, kennen Sie die Gestaop Hauptquartier?" The man nodded and Nolke turned back to Parker and the girl.

"You," he said to Sabine, "you can go, but I'll be seeing you again." And without waiting for an answer he opened the lorry door, shoved Parker in alongside the driver and then squeezed alongside him and told the driver to go.

• • •

"Now, my friend, I'll have your papers." Nolke stood over Parker as he sat in the chair alongside the table. Parker gave him the papers and sat silent. Nolke laid them on the table, bending over to examine them carefully. After a few minutes he walked over to the door and locked it.

"These are forged my friend, you're really in the shit. You'll get at least five years or deportation." He stared at Parker's impassive face and his fist came out so suddenly that Parker flinched even before the knuckles split his cheek. He could feel blood running down to his jaw but he didn't take his eyes off Nolke. If Nolke had been sure that his papers were forged he wouldn't have needed to use the rough stuff.

"What's your name?"

"Chaland. Charles Chaland."

"What's your work?"

"I service and repair agricultural machinery."

"Where were you going with the girl?"

"I hadn't decided."

"What's her name?"

And Parker knew by instinct that Nolke had just been trying a pick-up. The usual German approach. First the courteous German officer and then the tough guy. Parker gave no answer and Nolke's big fist blinded him as it crashed between his eyes.

"Who is she?"

"Go to hell." And Nolke's boot got him expertly under his knee-cap and he fought against unconsciousness. He felt as if the chair was falling backwards and as his head struck the floor he realized that it was. He was sprawled on his back alongside the desk, and Nolke stood over him, hands on hips. He tried to struggle up but the room tilted and he blacked out as he fell back.

When he came to Nolke was sitting at the desk drinking coffee. He barely glanced at Parker as he slowly stood up. Then as if he had just noticed Parker the German threw his identity card and his travel pass on the floor.

"In future don't interfere when a German officer is talking to a lady. I'll be looking out for you, my friend." He nodded his dismissal.

The cold air gripped him as he stood outside the building. It was obviously just before curfew, the late ones were hurrying home and the streets were almost empty. He steadied himself with one arm on a wall as he moved off slowly. At the corner he stopped, it seemed impossible to take another step and when a car stopped the noise of its brakes made him groan. And then the running footsteps and an arm round his shoulder. He swung slowly with his fist. He saw the cobbles coming up at his face and then it was over.

• • •

When he awoke he could see the moon through the tops of bare-branched trees, one eye was closed and the other quivered without stopping. A shadow fell across his face and a cold wet cloth touched his forehead as a girl's voice said, "Don't move." As he turned his head slightly he saw Bonnier crouching beside him, his breath clouding in the cold air.

"How'd you feel, chief?"

"Fine."

Bonnier gave a grunting laugh. "You don't look it. Can you eat? We've got a chicken, special donation from the locals. Try some chicken soup, chef's recommendation. The doc said when you wake up you've got to stay awake for at least four hours or the drugs'll keep you out for days."

Parker turned his head slowly and saw Sabine's serious face. The dark eyes watched him, and he realized that her arm was under his head, supporting him gently. He sighed with pain as he took a breath and blood came from his nose and mouth as he struggled to sit up.

When Bonnier and the girl lifted him so that he could drink the soup he saw that there were tears on Sabine's cheeks. When he lay back he closed his eyes and the girl's soft fingers stroked his face. "Stay awake, Charles. Look at the stars. The same stars are over England." Each time his eyes had closed her fingers had gently opened them. When, involuntarily, he had shivered, she took off her thick jacket and covered his body as best she could and the next time he was aroused from the edge of sleep he was conscious of his head cradled against the warm softness of her breasts.

By morning they had let him sleep and it was mid-day when he finally awoke. There was a watery sun shining and as he raised himself on one elbow he saw two of Bonnier's men with rifles standing guard over him a few metres away. When they saw that he was awake they had waved to him and turned to call a group of men in the distance.

A man in British army uniform came over. It was Tomkins, the training lieutenant who had been dropped with the Jedburgh team for Bonnier's maquis. He bent down full of concern.

"How are you, sir? They certainly gave you a bashing. Bonnier left orders for me to get you back to Puy Henry.

They're up there now, stocking you up with food and making the place ship-shape and all that." It seemed strange to hear English, and school-boy English at that.

Chapter Six

Frenez was waiting for him outside the station at Limoges. Neither acknowledged the other, but Parker kept Frenez in sight as they walked towards the river. At Pont St. Etienne, Frenez turned left and waited for Parker to catch up. There was a blustering wind that came off the river and Frenez stood with one hand trying to keep his fair hair from his eyes.

Parker had only met Frenez a few times before he had been recalled to Baker Street, and in those days Frenez was the leader of an independent reseau. Parker had only seen him once since his return. He was one of those men who Parker instinctively disliked. He had been an officer in the Chasseurs Alpins, he had a shrapnel scar on his left cheek and somehow it made him look even more raffishly handsome than he already was. Frenez was a lawyer in Limoges and moved among the bourgeoisie and the aristocrats with an ease and an indifference to their constraints that annoyed them as much as it annoyed the likes of Parker. Frenez's pale blue eyes missed nothing and the half smile that seemed permanently on his lips was all too frequently openly amused with a cynicism that was typical of the man. Frenez was always sure of himself and there were some who secretly would have liked to see just a second's touch of panic in those blue eyes. But the self-assurance was well founded, and the easy charm made it just tolerable.

"Who fixed your face, Chaland?"

"Nolke."

"He was up here last week. I've got a place for you tonight but I thought we'd be better off nearby here first. There are a lot of people for you to meet and I'd rather talk with you first. We can go to the water-bailiff's cottage." He nodded upstream and the old cottage was just visible. Frenez continued, "Let me go first and check."

"OK."

Parker kept a hundred metres behind Frenez and waited as Frenez turned down a path at the far side of the cottage. When he came out and waved, Parker walked over.

The water-bailiff was a small man whose eyes missed nothing and he was obviously impressed by his visitor. He moved to the old arm-chair and tactfully said that he needed to check the river levels and left them.

Frenez sat in his chair leaning forward, his whole body indicating his energy and impatience.

"Any objections to me having direct contact with London, Chaland?"

"None at all as long as you keep me in the picture."

"The messages I've had from you seem to want to hold us back."

"That's partly true. I don't want to stir up the Germans too early. Apart from the reprisals I don't want them to see a pattern of targets until it's too late for them to react effectively."

"What would you approve out of the list I sent you?"

"All the industrial targets and the rolling stock diversions where you can divert food or keep it in France. I'd like you to wreck both of the pylons and the sub-station at Chalus as soon as possible but I want a detailed account of what the Germans do about repairs. Timing, number of men, materials and all that."

"What about the other pylon targets?"

"I'll give you special instructions nearer the time, but do a thorough recce of all the sites on your list."

"It's a good group now for sabotage but we're badly off for weapons."

"I'll fix a drop for you."

"Anything else?"

"I'd like a plan of the prison, the Gestapo place and the SD place and all the details you can get of people and movements."

Frenez nodded. "Any idea when it's going to be—the landings?"

"No, André, and I've got to say the same to everybody—if I did know I couldn't say. But we'll fix an internal radio net quite soon. Late evening. No traffic if there's no news."

"I hear you got Lachaise away from the Germans."

"Yes."

"Any news of her?"

"We got her to Algiers alive. I've heard nothing since and I don't expect to hear."

"How d'you get on with Bonnier?"

"OK."

"I wouldn't trust those bastards, they're getting set to take over when it's all over."

"So is de Gaulle."

Frenez smiled a cold smile. "You don't have to worry, Chaland, you'll be back in London covered with medals."

"And you'll be pleading in court for the collaborators."

Frenez laughed. "Touché. I'll need all the business I can get. Half of Limoges classes me as a collaborator now."

"Why?"

"The Germans need advice from time to time on the Code Napoléon and they come to me for advice. They pay me well and they think I'm a good boy."

"London will straighten that out when it's all over."

"By the way, there are new documents for rations being issued next month. I've got advance copies—genuine and unused—if you want them for London."

"I'll take them back with me for the next Lysander trip."

"OK. I've got a communications problem at the moment."

"What's that?"

"Non-priority routine instructions. I've got twenty-three people I need to keep contact within the reseau and they're spread all round the countryside. I need three, maybe four, letter boxes and I haven't got one. Not a safe one anyway."

"I thought you were using the museum curator."

"He's got seven kids and the Germans are getting tough even with low-grade operators."

"Is he windy?"

"No. I just don't want him on my conscience."

"You'd better do what we do, use beehives."

"Beehives?"

"Yes, you stick the messages down the side of the tray. Nobody fiddles about with beehives."

Frenez grinned. "I like that, Chaland. Let's go back into town. You'll be staying out of town tonight at Oradour. The butcher there is one of ours. He'll be doing guard all night with his son. Your visit is the next best thing to having Charles de Gaulle in the parlour. Tout confort."

"And how are things with you yourself, André?"

Frenez looked up quickly, surprised, and he was silent for a moment before he answered.

"You must be the same, Chaland. I get tired of being the omniscient boss. The guy who has all the answers. I haven't had anybody ask how I feel about it all for years. I'm tired of standing up in court all day defending farmers who've played on the black market or offended some stupid new regulation from Vichy. I'm tired of playing Robin Hood for London. I'm tired of little parties given by the people who run this town. I hate their guts, next to the Germans. The bastards who can accommodate to anything." He sighed. "And I'm sick of myself. I don't like this patient waiting game. I'd like to walk into an SS officers' mess and just spray them with a machine-gun and call it a day."

"Would you like a week in London?"

Frenez leaned back, shaking his head and smiling. "Oh God no, all that trotting round the countryside and unarmed combat and map-reading. I didn't want to be a Boy Scout even when I was a kid."

"You don't have to go on a training course. Just a week's relaxation with real sleep."

"With some bloody RAF pilot risking his life so that I can screw some sweetie in London. He'd be sure to have seven kids, too. No, I'll just see it out, Charles. But thanks for asking. London never do."

"It's my job to ask, not theirs. What are you going to do after the war. Politics?"

"You're crazy, Charles." He leaned forward again, his eyes alight. "When it's over I'm going to Saigon and I'll have a villa covered with bougainvillaea and mimosa, and the three prettiest girls in town. One for me and two for the high-class clientele. Sunshine all day, every day, and I'll show the rich locals how to avoid income tax for large fees and I shall live happy ever after." And as he stood up smiling he was singing softly "La petite Tonkinoise," and Parker realized that he might actually mean what he said.

• • •

Parker had taken the train from Limoges early on the morning of the third day. Every carriage was packed and the corridors were solid with housewives heading for the farms. At the station just outside the fork at Nexon the train had stopped and many of the passengers got off. The train had stood there for ten minutes before they saw the reason for the delay. A German officer was shouting orders to a platoon of soldiers. They were lining the platform, and as Parker looked out of the window he saw others lining the track. It was twenty minutes before the sergeant and the corporal got to Parker's compartment. They checked the two women first and then the corporal reached for Parker's papers. He stood there, reading them slowly and carefully, When he had finished he looked at Parker and passed the papers to the sergeant. The sergeant read them equally carefully and then beckoned to Parker to follow him. As he got down on to the platform Parker saw that the whole area was thick with soldiers. There must have been fifty or more and they wouldn't be out in such numbers just for a routine check of a local train.

He was shown into a small office off a corridor. They had picked up about twenty men. Three or four were lined up farther down the corridor, and as Parker watched he saw another two joining them from another office and the sergeant looked briefly at their papers as he opened the door for them to walk out into the station yard. In the first office was a crowd of men all waiting to be checked and nobody spoke. After two or three had been ushered into the next office he saw them join the line in the corridor and pass the sergeant to go free.

The sergeant came for him and he was pushed into the inner office ahead of the others waiting. There was an officer of the Feldgendarmerie seated at a small table. Parker's papers were already in front of him. He stood there, in front of the table, as they went through the details on his identity card and his travel permit. When it was over the officer had leaned back looking at Parker intently.

"And why do you need a Fahrschein, Chaland?"

"Because of the area I have to cover."

"To do what. Spy for the English?"

"Herr Leutnant, I service farm machinery and I don't imagine the English would be very interested in the state of tractors and balers in the Haute-Vienne."

"There are other things, my friend. Anyway what are you doing up here?"

"This is part of my area, Herr Leutnant."

"What were you doing in Limoges?"

"I came to check a tractor and its accessories."

"What accessories?"

"A plough, a harrow, a baler and a muck-spreader."

"Why are you travelling on forged papers, Chaland?"

"They're not forged, monsieur. They were issued by the authorities."

"And who was the lucky farmer who enjoyed your services to a tractor?"

"Firadoux. La Ferme des Brumes at les Allois."

The lieutenant gave him a cold smile.

"You realize we shall check?"

"But of course, m'sieur."

"Good. Wait in the next office."

"May I ask, m'sieur, which paper you think is forged?"

"Maybe both, but certainly the travel permit."

"May I have my identity paper, Herr Leutnant, it is an offence to be without."

The lieutenant handed him the identity paper and passed the travel permit to a soldier clerk.

"Check the address he gave. If in doubt bring the farmer Firadoux in for questioning."

Parker had been shoved into the adjoining office. There was one other man sitting there. He was visibly shaking. Parker waited for five minutes and then slowly walked to the door that gave on to the corridor. And down the corridor to the far end where he walked to the door and joined the short queue whose papers the sergeant was cursorily checking.

When it was Parker's turn the sergeant put his head sideways to look at the identity papers and nodded him out towards the open door. As Parker walked through the door into the pale spring sunshine there was a pen of sheep over to his left and the cobbled station yard sloped down to a picket fence and narrow gate flanked by a tracklayer's hut. As he headed for the open gate the temptation to look back to the station building was almost overwhelming. There was a German soldier with his rifle slung on his shoulder standing alongside the gate. When Parker proffered his papers the soldier shook his head and waved him on.

As the road sloped away and curved to the left there was a huddle of industrial buildings. There was a layer of white dust everywhere and several railway trucks piled high with chunks of limestone. There were three cycles leaning together under a framework of corrugated iron. A thin chain linked their frames and the angle iron of the building. Parker pulled the outside cycle until the chain was fully stretched. Then, with a sharp jerk, he snapped the chain and the cycle came free.

Without glancing backwards he mounted the cycle and let it free-wheel down the slope of the road. One hundred metres farther on a small road was signed Champagnac and he swung off to the left and pedalled furiously. The small road branched again after three kilometres and he took the road marked Brouillet. Just before the junction to St. Maurice he saw the row of cottages and he stopped. He hid the cycle in the hedge and walked slowly along the lane. There was an old woman standing at the door of the first cottage. She was waving a letter in her hand. He walked up the short path. She looked at him with her head held back and her eyes half closed.

"Is that young Martin?"

"I'm afraid not, madame. Can I help you?"

"There was this letter this morning. I want to know what it says."

"Shall I open it and read it to you?"

"Ah, m'sieur, that would be kind. Young Martin must be away. The postman always tells him when a letter comes." She offered him the envelope and he slit it open with his finger. And the old lady said, "Come inside, we can sit down together and enjoy it."

His eyes saw the censorship stamp and the prison commandant's stamp. The address was Fresnes Prison in Paris. And as he silently read the text he heard footsteps running up the garden path and he moved quickly to stand against the long curtain at the door. The door was flung open and a young man stood there breathless, looking slowly round the room. Parker stepped out from behind the door.

"Are you Martin?"

The boy swung around. "Yes. Who are you? Have you read her the letter?"

"Not yet."

"Give it to me. I'll read it to her."

Parker handed over the letter and the young man read it silently and then started to speak:

"Chere maman—I am very well—the job is well paid—I have good food—I am very busy—Paris looks beautiful these days—all my love, Solange."

He looked aggressively at Parker and folded up the letter and put it in his pocket. The old lady stood up slowly.

"Would the gentleman like some soup?"

"I should be very grateful, madame."

She walked along feeling the wall towards the kitchen, and when she had gone the youth said, "It would kill her if she knew. We pretend that Solange was ordered by the Germans to work in Paris."

"And why is she in Fresnes?"

"The Germans said she was a courier for the Resistance."

"And was she?"

The shrewd peasant eyes ignored his glance. "Who knows, m'sieur, these are strange times."

"Who arrested her, the Gestapo or the SD?"

"The milice from Salignac. The bloody undertaker."

"Why should he do that?"

"He wanted her. She was pretty and the Gestapo offered a reward for all Resistance people. He sold her for 1,000 francs." He turned to look at Parker defiantly. "He was shot in the stomach two days later. Took a nice long time to die."

Parker looked at the youth. "I need some help from you, Martin."

"What kind of help?"

"The Germans are looking for me now. They'll be combing the area for me. I need somewhere to hide and I need a message got to Périgueux."

The young man stared at Parker's face and said quietly: "My God, I've heard about you. You're the Englishman who was in the Corrèze. You got beaten up by the Germans. Sure I'll help you. Anybody in these cottages would help you. You come with me."

• • •

It was three hours before the Germans came. Twenty men and dogs, and the little in-heat bitch sheepdog that one of the villagers had fetched from the farm at Jurignac kept the tracker dogs in turmoil. Parker lay in one of the big field drains and apart from being soaked to the skin there were no problems. It was Devereux who came for him on one of Bonnier's motorcycles the next day.

CHAPTER SEVEN

Devereux had bad news. The Abwehr had moved into Périgueux and the indications were that there was to be an all out campaign against the Resistance, and in particular they had put top priority on the capture of Parker. There were posters going up in the area offering 100,000 francs reward for information leading to Parker's arrest. There was no name on the poster but there was a police artist's sketch that was recognizably Parker.

Back at the cottage at Puy Henry Parker had spent the evening reading his copies of the signals traffic from the three reseaux and two things were clear. The German counter-intelligence services were stepping up their action in the area against the Resistance and Parker's groups were losing morale because of his instructions to hold back.

Sabine had brought a message from Bonnier. His maquisards were growing in number and they needed more arms and more ammunition urgently. The Germans were mounting patrols against them now so that they had to keep on the move all the time. They were up on the plateau that even the locals called "le bout du monde." He looked up from the paper to the girl. "I need a night's sleep, Sabine. We'll cycle over to Bonnier tomorrow. You'd better stay."

The girl had tidied up the rooms and dusted the place while Parker sat with maps and his notebook, and at six o'clock he had suggested that they go to Brantôme for a meal. But she said she couldn't face the Germans unless she had to. She got them a meal and tuned the old-fashioned bakelite radio to the BBC French service and turned it low and listened. Almost at the end of the message was the clearance for the drop for the reseau in the Corrèze. "Le chat qui rit est ici." The drop would be the next night near Argentat. The girl was watching his face. Apart from the twitching muscles under the bruising around his eye she saw the tell-tale white streaks at his mouth that signalled his exhaustion, and the strain was all too obvious around the eyes.

"Why not sleep long tomorrow, Charles. You need rest if you're to carry on."

He turned his head slowly to look at her. "There was a message for us on the radio. There's to be a drop tomorrow night. I'll have to organize them."

"Devereux could do that."

"It's not in his area, it's for my old reseau at Brive. I should see them anyway."

"Well go to bed now."

"I need to sit up until curfew time in case anyone comes."

"I could do that."

He smiled. "You'd never be able to wake me."

"We'll see."

He stood up slowly and wearily.

"You're going to make somebody a wonderful mother."

She blushed and went out to the primitive kitchen, and after a few minutes he followed her and sat on a stool as she bent over the sink. It reminded him of the kitchen at Victoria Road. The china clay sink, the wooden draining-board, a string line to take dishcloths, aprons and towels. And the woman at the sink, her back bent, her hands moving a cloth on a blue-patterned plate and the naked bulb hanging from the ceiling where the gas lamp had been at his home. It would have been let to others after his mother had died, and maybe the faded huntsmen who galloped across the old wallpaper in the hall had already been replaced. It was his home no more, neither was anywhere else. But he had a strange, warm feeling of security sitting in the kitchen while the girl worked.

At midnight he went upstairs to bed and as the girl followed she was surprised to hear him whistling softly. She had only seen him smile once in all the time she had known him and she had never seen any signs of pleasure or even relaxation: his mind never strayed from his work, and his interest in people was confined to their contribution to the Resistance. And long weeks ago she had known that she loved him. But her own personality was almost as narrow as his own. The emotions were there but they were seldom demonstrated. Even after the night when he had rescued her from Nolke he had never referred to the incident again and she had been too shy even to thank him. But she knew by instinct that he knew that she was grateful.

He had lit one of the precious candles for her in the small bedroom and nodded to her as he left. An hour later, still awake, she had got up and walked along the short passage. His door was open and the moonlight splashed across his face. He lay on his back and she looked at his face. Bonnier had said that Devereux had told him that Chaland was twenty-three or twenty-four. He looked an old man now, his eyes black sockets in the deep shadow from the moonlight, his cheeks hollow and the skin over his nose drawn tight. One naked arm hung down to trail on the floor. Despite the coolness of the night there was sweat beaded on his forehead and along the edge of his jaw. And if it hadn't been for the sweat he could have been a corpse.

She knelt down quietly and very gently her hand touched his forehead and she was shocked by its coldness. When she moved her hand he sighed and spoke slowly, with long pauses as if he were drugged. "Bonnier's group . . . is far too big . . . it's got to be . . . broken down . . . into small units . . . and then . . ." And his lips stopped moving and he turned uneasily towards the wall. She sat beside him for an hour. Everything was still and silent in the night until far away a church clock struck two and she went back to her bed.

• • •

They had cycled together the next morning to meet Bonnier at Nontron. The meeting was in the private office of a small shoe factory whose owner, Langlois, was part of the new reseau based in Périgueux. He was a mild, gentle man with the air of a schoolmaster, but appearances belied the facts. Langlois had led six-man teams on fifteen sabotage missions and his men were efficient and disciplined.

Parker, Bonnier, Langlois and the girl sat around the old-fashioned desk and Parker had started in straightaway.

"Bonnier your group is far too big. It's going to get out of control if you don't reorganize. You've got to clip it down into groups of no more than a hundred. That will give you the chance to promote some of your good types and you can spread yourselves over a wider area. It's too easy for the Germans to find a big group like yours, you become an artillery target, and apart from that it will keep your men occupied while you're sorting out."

Bonnier shrugged. "We could give the Germans a run for their money right now."

"Sure you could. And what would be the result. Heavy losses for your men, terrible counter-measures by the Germans on the whole area, and you'd have shown your strength. Next time they tackled you they'd have armour and artillery, and they'd not only wipe you out but they would reduce to rubble every village they went through."

"How long do we have to wait, Chaland? London keeps you in the picture but nobody tells us anything. When will the landings be? Will they even be this year?"

Parker looked across at Bonnier. "Get Lieutenant Tomkins to train three really good reception teams and I'll arrange a big arms drop. We'll be able to do that next moon, just another four weeks. We'll need three or four drop zones for three successive nights, so spread them out. And those will be the last drops of arms you get before you use them."

The others sat silent, aware of the significance of what Parker had said. Finally Bonnier had spoken.

"OK, Chaland. We'll do as you say. But I'll believe it when it happens."

Parker's eyes half-closed in momentary anger as he looked at Bonnier.

"You and your men would still be running round with a dozen World War I rifles and a few pitchforks if it hadn't been for London. No doubt you get your marching orders from Moscow but if it was left to them you'd rot."

Langlois had seen the resentment on Bonnier's face and he leaned forward. "Michel, in a short while we shall all have so much to do. We must spend the time in-between preparing. The landings will only be the start, our part in harassing the Germans will be vital."

Bonnier had stood up, and beckoning to Sabine, he had left.

Langlois turned to Parker. "Charles, Bonnier has great pressure on him. The Communists want to take over when France is liberated. They could do it, and maybe they will. The times are terrible now but when it is over then we could have civil war and Resistance men will be fighting on different sides. But keep us together until it's over, Charles, otherwise the sacrifices have been too great."

Parker banged the desk with his fist. "Langlois, when the Germans are under pressure from the invasion they are going to show no mercy. The harassment the Resistance gets now is nothing to what we will get in a few months time. And not just us. They'll kill civilians without mercy. If Bonnier's people stir them up now the civilian population will be against us."

"Maybe you're right, Charles, but don't be too sure."

Parker put both hands flat on the desk as if that would dismiss the argument. He looked up at Langlois. "I went up for a meeting with Frenez. On the train coming back there was a special check. Fifty or sixty Germans. They were looking for somebody special. It wasn't routine. And there are posters up in Périgueux offering a reward for my capture. Somebody's keeping the Germans informed. Any idea who it could be?"

Langlois leaned back in his big chair. "Has Frenez lost any men to the Germans recently?"

"Yes, four, but they were all killed."

"Sure?"

"Yes."

"Did they all die immediately?"

"I don't know."

"They would happily torture a man while he was dying, my friend."

"Any other ideas?"

"The girl you rescued. Lachaise, the radio operator. She could have talked in the end. And who is in charge of your old reseau in the Corrèze?"

"Heriot."

"Jules Heriot?"

"Yes."

"The man who owns the brick-works?"

"That's the one."

Langlois sighed. "I find it impossible to see anyone in the Resistance as a traitor. Maybe someone could be insecure, could talk too much. But a traitor no. They have no need to join."

Parker pursed his lips. "You're too nice a man, Langlois. For me anyone could be a traitor. All it needs is the right pressure."

"And what would be the right pressure on me?"

"Your wife, that pretty daughter."

Langlois shook his head. "Not even for them would I talk. Anyway, I should know they would kill them even if I did talk."

"Have you checked all the pylon sites?"

"Yes. No problems."

"And the railway targets?"

"We've covered them up to Angoulême and to Limoges, after that Frenez's team take over. One request though."

"What's that?"

"You remember you gave us a demonstration of those little tire bursters. We could do with a lot of those."

"They've promised to let me have more but they're having difficulty making enough. Any other problems?"

Langlois smiled. "None that I can't cope with,"

"Could you manage another six teams?"

"Sure."

"Do that then. Recruit carefully."

• • •

He had a rendezvous in Périgueux with Devereux that evening, and as he walked down the street he saw a man on the opposite side of the road watching the café. He was wearing a raincoat and the skies were pale blue and the sun was strong for a spring evening. Only German security men wore raincoats on a warm spring evening. Parker walked past the café. Devereux was sitting at one of the tables reading a paper and there were five or six other people at various tables. They had frequently met at the café and it looked as if someone had tipped off the Germans. The net was closing in on him, or on Devereux.

He walked back past the café so that he could make certain that Devereux had seen him. The watcher was still there and looking at his watch as if he were expecting to be relieved. Devereux and he had both played these games at Beaulieu, and he walked back to the centre of the town. He left a message for Devereux with the woman at the cash desk of the cinema. And he left a second message that would give the garage address with the porter at the Hotel Domino.

It was two hours later when Devereux arrived and he had changed his clothes meantime to workmen's overalls.

"You're sure you've not been tailed?"

"I was tailed all right. There were two of them but I gave them the slip at the cathedral. I went back to my place and changed."

"Any idea who they were?"

"They were Nolke's men. One's a German and the other's Belgian."

"Who were they looking for?"

"Must be you, chief. I was there and if they knew me they'd have picked me up."

"They could have been waiting to see who your contacts were or trail you back to where you live."

"I've moved again, chief. I'm at the butcher's place."

Parker looked at his watch: "We haven't got long until curfew. How are your group?"

"You've seen the radio traffic with London?"

"Yes. Your stuff is too long. You've been on the air for twenty minutes three nights out of five. Did the girl agree?"

"Yes."

"Well tell 'Toinette from me that in future it's ten minutes at the outside. This place is too small. If they really start looking, they'll pick her up in a week."

Devereux nodded. "We've done two locomotives with that grease they dropped. They did about ten kilometres and then ground to a stand-still. The people at the sheds say that repairs will take six months."

"What's the position with vegetables?"

"There's just potatoes now. Two wagon loads a day go off to Germany. We've organized the farmers and as soon as the Boche wagons are loaded they get a hundred kilos of rotting potatoes at the half-way point. The farmers say that three-quarters of the load will be rotten by the time they arrive."

"Any chance of directing German loads back here?"

"No. We haven't done that for a month. They're watching all freight like hawks. The last time they found a truck on the sidings they executed the foreman and two workers at Angoulême. They had nothing to do with it. It was us. I've stopped it. We can start again when it all happens."

"How's 'Toinette?"

"She's OK."

Parker sensed the second's hesitation. "Except for what?"

"She's moved in with her fellow."

"Did you give her permission?"

"Yes."

"You knew I had forbidden it?"

"Yes, chief, but she's desperate for some security. There have been three raids by the Germans on the garage in the last two weeks. The fellow helps where we can't."

Parker's voice was cold. "You'd better get on your way, Jean-Luc, I'll contact you the day after tomorrow."

• • •

Parker had coded his messages and transmitted them on the early morning schedule and had slept at 2 a.m. and was awake at 5 a.m. He had two farm jobs to do that day. His latest receipt was three weeks old. His background wouldn't stand up to a serious interrogation without more actual work being recorded. He had to cover a wide area for repair work because the Dordogne farms had little need for farm machinery. There was an old saying about Dordogne farms—"un peu de tout," because of the peasant caution that made them grow strips of a dozen crops from potatoes to tobacco. There were critics outside the Dordogne who said it was more like "beaucoup de rien." But the farmers of the Périgord had survived the "Alemans" who had destroyed the city in A.D. 276 and the Romans before them, and their piece-meal crops gave variety to their work and variety to their diets, and tractors and machinery were seen as hostages to fortune. And the Périgord had produced Montaigne as well as its peasants.

Chapter Eight

It had taken two weeks to arrange the dropping zones for Bonnier's maquisards and it was the the end of April before the moon and the weather were suitable.

The Gestapo had been up to the Comte's manor house and had searched the main building and the out-buildings for two days, leaving a guard overnight. They found nothing.

Baker Street had been critical of Parker's close liaison with Bonnier and his group, but they had accepted his requests for more arms and ammunition. Parker had the feeling that their criticism was for the record, and that unofficially they approved his actions. In the same signals traffic had been the official notification of his promotion to major, taking effect 1 Jan 44.

By mid-May the training had begun to pay off. The three reseaux had laid down good communications between them and detailed plans had been made for the sabotage of hundreds of targets. Parker was working his radio back to London from the room in Périgueux.

As if there were literally something in the air there was

talk everywhere of an Allied invasion. There were rumours of landings on the Mediterranean coast and at Bordeaux, and even when the rumours were proved to be unfounded morale stayed high. Parker had warned all concerned to take it for granted that the talk of landings was being put around by the Germans in the hope of the Resistance showing its hand prematurely. An arms drop south of Limoges that Parker had arranged for Frenez had been only partially successful. Almost a quarter of the supplies had been collected by the Germans.

On 20 May a group of Bonnier's maquis had disobeyed orders and had attacked a German column in the steep hills just north of St. Pardoux. They caught the Germans in what looked like a perfect ambush, a narrow road flanked by deeply wooded steep hills on each side with tree trunks across the road to halt the vehicles. But they had learned their first expensive lesson. The Germans had accepted the challenge and had carried out a ruthless, angry, destruction patrol that left twenty-five of Bonnier's men dead and seven badly wounded before the Germans went on their way north. The Germans lost ten men and a burnt out scout-car. The lesson was that if you corner fighting troops and cut off their route of advance you have to leave it at that. If you want to take pot shots at an armoured column you must expect to pay a high price for your bravery or stupidity. They also learned that although Sten guns look good and feel good they are hopelessly inaccurate against single targets.

Politics were beginning to intrude into the fabric of the Resistance, and London ordered Parker to use extreme caution with Bonnier. It was now the official line of the French Communist Party to denigrate all resistance operations controlled from London, and to start up a propaganda campaign against all the remnants of pre-war authority in French politics and community life. It was becoming disturbingly clear that the Communists had no loyalties except to Moscow. But Bonnier still accepted Parker's orders and there was no reluctance in his co-operation.

Baker Street informed Parker of the formation of de Gaulle's FFI and that the frictions between de Gaulle and the British Government were being transferred to the field of the

Resistance. Brave Frenchmen who had risked their lives for years were pushed aside at de Gaulle's headquarters and in the field, for men who preferred hierarchies to action. There were half a dozen different organizations to which the population in France could adhere, and the Communists had penetrated them all except the networks of SOE.

Bonnier had transferred Sabine to Parker's small headquarter staff to act as courier to his maquis and to the leaders of the three reseaux under Parker's command.

On the evening of 3 June Parker had been sitting with Bonnier, Sabine, Devereux and Frenez in the farm cottage at Puy Henry. They had come in from the heat of the small garden, and with only two chairs in the small room they were sitting on the floor with their backs to the wall listening to the BBC French service. Parker had a feeling that that day would be the start, and he had listened intently to the messages. When the announcer said "Les lauriers sont coupés" he made no sign of recognition, but when the second warning came of "Les absents ont toujours tort" it was more than he could do to hold back the news. He stood up, turned off the radio and held up his hand. There was no need for more to get their attention.

"My friends, the waiting is over. Some time in the next ten days we shall receive our order to attack the many targets we have identified. I must emphasize that nothing will be done beyond last-minute reconnaissance and preparation until I tell you. If that order is disobeyed the invasion could fail. The Germans will know that the landings are imminent. I shall see you all in the next ten days but I want to say now that London relies on this circuit to play its part in fighting the Germans in the way we know best. Sabotage and harassment. There will be room for a thousand heroes and they will have my every support, but we are fighting a grim battle—the odds are hundreds to one against us and the Germans will have no mercy, and they will no longer need to pretend. Bonnier, Devereux, go back to your men—Frenez, you will stay here tonight." He turned to Sabine. "Sabine—a bottle."

And they had drunk their toasts and thought their own thoughts, and gone. Their excitement was barely contained.

Only Parker seemed unaffected by the news. He had sat in the garden with Frenez and Sabine, watching the sun go down across the valley. He felt a great peace in his mind that the time of real action was so near. He wondered when he would get the message ordering him to carry out the special operation that was to be his alone. There would be the special BBC message and the next radio signal that he would receive would be in a special code for him alone.

• • •

Frenez left early the next morning and Parker had cycled down to Périgueux, and as if to bring all concerned a cautionary tale Baker Street had sent a signal listing the cover names of nine SOE agents in Paris and the Zone Occupée who had been captured in the previous month. Their circuits were no longer to be considered secure. Parker had never contacted any of the ZO SOE reseaux but he had heard talk of them at Wanborough Manor and Beaulieu, and they were rated as highly experienced people. What could happen in the north had happened in his area too.

There was no longer any need to back his cover story with any actual agricultural repair work. He could get receipts from a hundred farmers that would give him all the cover he needed.

He and Sabine had sat listening that night to the BBC broadcast. There were long lists of messages but none were for him. They had played chess on a pocket set until midnight and she had won every game although she doubted if he had noticed. And, as always now, he sat in the kitchen as she did her work.

It was the next evening when the release messages were broadcast, and as he heard them come over the air he knew from their text that all over France the SOE men would know that one kind of war was over and a new one was about to begin. And in London Churchill had summoned Charles de Gaulle to inform him that the next night would see the launching of D-day to be fought on a plan the Frenchman had never seen, and on which he had not been consulted.

Parker had cycled to Périgueux and used Devereux's

courier to pass his orders to Angoulême, Limoges and Brive. The only two objectives now were to help take some of the pressure from the Allied troops in the north and to harass the German troops who would be drawn up from the south as reinforcements. The Germans would be fighting on French soil but from now on they would be fighting for their survival and the survival of Germany. It would be a bitter struggle. Even more bitter here behind the lines than in the battle area.

Parker had monitored all the BBC programmes on the 5th June but on the morning of the 6th he had missed the statement by Eisenhower about the Allied landings. It was mid-morning before he learned that the landings had started. Twenty-four hours later than expected. He had sent couriers to Brive, Limoges and to Bonnier in the hills above St. Yrieix-La-Perche. He had gone himself to Périgueux. That afternoon two SS divisions had moved into his area and the public exhilaration had quickly turned to fear. The civil population were treated with open hostility now, and the French traitors of the Milice were denouncing as members of the Resistance all those whom they hated or envied, and in fields and town squares the SS men executed the innocent and the guilty "pour encourager les autres."

On his mid-day radio net to London, Baker Street ordered a special concentration on the crack SS division Das Reich which was moving up from the south to Normandy. Parker specified the targets and the attack plan with the group at Brive and headed north to Limoges to get Frenez's men alerted for their part against the SS division. He sent a courier to Bonnier ordering him to cut the N21 road and the N20 at as many places as the maquis could cover. He used Frenez's new radio operator to send his radio traffic to London. For two days and nights Parker moved around the Limoges area planning the sabotage patrols and the snipers. When the Das Reich division got thirty kilometres outside Limoges they would be out of Parker's area and others would carry the load, but he intended to show what could be done by determined men.

Frenez had shaken him awake mid-morning of the 8th.

"Chaland. There's a courier from Devereux."

Parker sat on the side of his bed as the young man spoke.

"Monsieur, Devereux sent me up to tell you that the Germans have come to a complete halt at Souillac. They won't be up here for another twenty-four hours."

"And casualities on our side?"

"Two men killed. They used cannon on us. At least seven Germans killed and some wounded."

"How did you hold them?"

"We mined the roads in ten places at hundred-metre intervals. They've got armoured vehicles stuck down the holes and they can't get the recovery vehicles up the road. They're having to dismantle them."

"What about the rest of the programme?"

"All the pylons are down except those at Brive. They're guarded by SS. The railway line is out at Sarlat and Gourdon. We shall blow up the line at Gramont when the Germans move on."

Parker sat naked at the rough table and scribbled a note to Devereux. His depression was lifting and he was beginning to catch the feeling of elation and excitement that the others had had for days.

• • •

At Chalus, the next day, they watched the SS Das Reich columns cross the village square and take the N701 road and halt for breakfast just outside the town. The forward patrol had finished their meal by the time the rear-guard had arrived. They were moving cautiously, and a spotter plane was slowly criss-crossing the area ahead of them on the main road.

Parker and Frenez had taken their men north of Chalus up the road to three kilometres south of Oradour-sur-Vayres. They assembled the men along the crest of the hill on the south side of the road. There were twenty men in the party but Parker had sent most of them off to blow the culvert just north of Oradour. There were five left for the ambush, including Frenez and Parker.

It was a hot morning, and as they looked across the landscape there was a heat mist coming up from the fields where the cattle stood knee deep in the small steams lined with poplars that fed back to the lake at La Pouge. They had sent a man to the village to warn everybody to stay indoors.

The look-out's messenger boy had come panting over the hill to them just before mid-day. The forward patrols of SS Division Das Reich were a kilometre away.

Parker had checked the Bren a dozen times already but from some reflex his left hand reached forward yet again and turned the wooden handle on the barrel and rammed it back in place. Without looking his fingers checked the catch and left it set at single shots. His right hand touched the magazine in the grass alongside the gun and tapped the other magazine on top of the breech as if it might be loose.

The slope of the hill was thick with buttercups and in the shallow dip where they lay the white heads of cow-parsley gave them cover. Parker pulled the gun back gently against the springs of the bipod and put his eye to the sight. There was no wind and the range was set for 500 metres. The road was a little farther away but there would be a fall in the trajectory to allow for. And then they came. A squadron of eight motorcyclists followed by four scout cars. The motorcyclists rode slowly, so slowly that they had to weave to keep their balance as they scanned both sides of the road. Two of them stopped and propped up their motorcycles on their stands and stood checking the slope of the hill with field glasses. Then came the troop carriers and trucks, their canvas covers down and machine-guns mounted on the metal framework. Parker watched carefully through his binoculars. The troops sat with rifles at the ready, and as he looked down the road he could see the dust from the long column as it spread over three kilometres down the road until it was hidden from sight by a spur of the hill.

Parker focused his glasses on a gate at the bend of the road and waited for a suitable target. He didn't want to attack until at least the forward patrol was past their ambush. Then he saw what he wanted. A fresh-faced blond German with the insignia of a Sturmbannführer. He was talking to his driver as he sat back in his open car. He was watching the road and he had a Luger in his right hand and his left hand held the windscreen frame to steady his ride. Parker said:

"The blond pig in the car in two minutes. I'll fire first. Just one magazine each and we scatter. I'll see you in Limoges at six tonight."

Parker pressed the long grass back on each side of the gun barrel and lifted the stock to his shoulder, slid the catch up to continuous fire, lined up the blond German in the sights and squeezed the trigger. The car's windscreen went white and the black-uniformed officer half stood and fell back, and the car hit the ditch and went on its side. Then Parker swung the gun to the left and traversed it along two troop lorries then back to the halted vehicles behind the car. A tanker went up in a burst of black smoke and then he saw men jumping from the carriers. As he got up on all fours he pulled back the bipod and smelt the grass burning as the hot barrel came down. Then crouching, he scrambled down the slope. The gun bouncing against his right leg as he ran. He fell again and again in his headlong rush. The van was there and he threw the gun into the back and started the engine. When he got to the N699 he turned and went down the main road to St. Mathieu then off up the back roads to the road alongside the river. An hour later he was in Rochechouart heading due east for Limoges. He left the Bren at the farm at les Bouchats and the van at the laundry near the cathedral. He waited for Frenez at his offices. He came an hour later. Clean, elegant and brief-case in hand. His secretary handed him the day's post and Frenez waved him into his private office.

He sat at his desk grinning. "My God, but that was good. They won't be untangling that lot for ten hours at least. And I've just seen Josef, they brought down the two pylons this morning and they've blown up the main line tunnel at Condat."

"There are two more SS divisions in the area, André, so watch out. They'll be very jumpy."

"To hell with them, Charles, today we hit their élite, "la crême de la crême"— Hitler's own."

"Have you got a radio?"

Frenez stood up and turned the brass knob on the old-fashioned safe in the wall. He took out a small Blaupunkt radio and stooped to plug it in. He tuned to the BBC. It was almost the end of the news bulletin and in the round-up when it was ending it said that Allied troops were attacking Caen and the Russians had taken Minsk and 100,000 German prisoners. Frenez stood up and put the radio back in the safe. He leaned, smiling, against the wall.

"It's unbelievable, Charles. It's actually going to happen."

"Where did you get the radio?"

"From a grateful German client."

"Who?"

"A lieutenant, an infantry lieutenant, stationed in Limoges."

"Why was he a client?"

"He'd got a local girl pregnant and she was bringing a paternity order against him. He was shit-scared his commanders would find out."

"What did you do?"

"Told the girl to drop it, and she did."

"A French girl?"

"Of course, my friend. It'll teach her not to open her legs for bloody Germans." He moved to his desk and sat down. "I wondered when you'd raise the subject, Charles."

"What subject?"

"The subject of who tipped off the Germans when you were here last time."

"Qui s'excuse, s'accuse."

Frenez smiled. "No, sir. I didn't say it wasn't me. It wasn't. But I didn't say so."

"Who do you think it was?"

Frenez leaned back in his chair as he looked at Parker.

"I think it was those oafs in London you play games with."

"That's ridiculous."

Frenez looked at him. "How old are you, Charles?"

"Twenty-five."

"Well let me teach you a lesson. The difference between a half-Frenchman and a real Frenchman. You're not a fool and I'd say you don't trust anybody. And I don't blame you, I don't either. But you *do* trust 'things.' Your superiors, organizations, that sort of thing. And that's where you make a mistake."

"Go on."

"I've got a little present for you, my friend." And he stood up and went back to the safe. He took out a sheet of paper and closed the safe door before sitting back at his desk. He read the paper silently as Parker waited. Then he looked up.

"You know I've never been on any of your British training courses. And never met the people. I was recruited in the field and I've just got on with it."

Parker nodded. Frenez looked down at the sheet of paper as he spoke.

"Your people operate out of offices in Baker Street. There are two sections. One is 'F' section, one is 'RF' section. 'RF' section holds hands with de Gaulle's people. 'F' section uses Britishers with French connections.

"You do training at Wanborough Manor, just outside Guildford, you do unarmed combat and commando training in Scotland near Inverness. And you do your agent's training at a place called Beaulieu, the home of an English milord.

"You work for 'F' section and your chief's name is Buckmaster, a lieutenant-colonel. Your operation here has the code-name 'Lantern' and your signals code name is Georges."

Frenez looked up at Parker's grim face, and waited.

"Where did you get that?"

Frenez leaned forward pushing back a loose lock of blond hair.

"This came from Paris. From the Gestapo in Paris to the Gestapo in Lyons, and from there to the Gestapo in Limoges. In the last two months the Paris Gestapo have arrested and interrogated nine men and two women. All SOE agents."

"How did you get hold of it?"

Frenez shook his head. "I'm nearly old enough to be your father, Chaland, and I'm nobody's fool. Where I got it is my business, but believe me they've got a lot more than this. And it doesn't all come from Paris. Some of it's local."

"Who?"

Frenez shrugged. "I don't know. I've got ideas. You must do your sums yourself."

"Can you phone Devereux to fetch me?"

"Sure I can. But not from this office."

• • •

Devereux had picked him up a couple of hours later and they drove straight back to Périgueux. In the early evening he had driven to Brive to talk to the reseau leaders about the next day's work. There were two road-blocks on the way but the chain-harrow in the back of the van had seen him through both of them.

He was back at Puy Henry at ten o'clock, and after they had eaten he walked along the ridge of the hill with Sabine and they sat in the dusk looking across the valley. There was the scent of clover and stocks on the evening air and it was tempting to look across the lush fields and imagine that the war was a figment of a tired mind.

While he was in Périgueux he had signalled London about the SOE leak and had added a bitter demand for clarification. His signal had been acknowledged without comment. Elated as he had been with the attack on the SS at Oradour-sur-Vayres, Frenez's news had depressed him deeply. He turned to the girl.

"Did you pass the messages to Bonnier today?"

She nodded. "Yes. His news was not good."

"Oh. Tell me."

"They attacked a German column near Thiviers. They killed some Germans and blew up some vehicles. The Germans went after them and used artillery. Bonnier lost a lot of men."

"How many?"

"Almost a hundred dead and fifty wounded."

"For Christ's sake. I warned him enough times. These are trained soldiers they're taking on."

The girl was silent and he saw her shiver.

"Anything else?"

"I'm afraid there is."

"Go on."

"The Gestapo man saw me in Périgueux. He stopped me and asked for my papers."

"So?"

"He wants to sleep with me."

Parker looked at the girl's face and realized that he'd never seen her as a girl who men would want to sleep with. Not because he hadn't found her attractive but because his own thoughts had been of work and comradeship.

"What did you do?"

"I said I would see him tomorrow evening."

"Did he ask where you live?"

"Yes. I said I lived at Lemaire's garage. It was stupid but I was frightened. He walked back with me there to check and Lemaire saw what was happening and backed up my story. He's picking me up there at nine tomorrow."

"How do you know he wants to sleep with you?"

She half-smiled. "Gestapo officers don't pick up French girls to hold hands. And apart from that he said so."

"What did he say?"

"He said he'd wanted me from the first time he saw me, that he had been looking for me. He said he could make things difficult for me if I didn't co-operate."

"And what are you going to do?"

She shrugged. "I'll sleep with him. If I don't he'll arrest everybody at the garage, and he'll hunt me down and I'll be arrested too. He'll have me one way or another. He's had other girls the same way. They killed one girl. One girl left the town and went to Paris and he arrested her parents and had them deported. They're in Belsen now."

He looked at the soft brown eyes and the full mouth, and saw them for the first time as other men saw them. She was wearing a silk blouse and he could see the fulness of her breasts and the brown skirt emphasized her long shapely legs. Her head was resting on her drawn-up knees, and he could see the whiteness of her small even teeth as she smiled at him. He turned to look across the valley but it was dark now, and away off to the north he could hear the drone of heavily laden bombers. He suddenly felt more alone than he had ever felt in his life. Frenez had taken away a piece of his security that morning. London were not to be relied on. And now the girl was no longer the girl who washed up in the kitchen, but a girl desired by men. It was enough for one day and Parker stood up and held out his hand to the girl to help her stand up. It was small and firm and warm, and he held it all the way back to the cottage.

• • •

Parker had had trouble starting the van but they were in Brive by eleven and back at Périgueux at mid-day. He had phoned Lemaire at the garage from a call-box in a café and for the first time he had given him the address of his room in the town.

Sabine had sat patiently as he encoded his messages for London, and when Lemaire had come Parker had put the pad in his inside pocket.

"Do your people know where you are, Lemaire?"

"Yes. I gave Mason this address in case anybody wanted to contact you. They're all on edge because of that Gestapo bastard."

"That's OK. Sit down."

When Lemaire had eased his big frame on to the small chair Parker had looked at him intently before he spoke.

"There's a farm just outside Brantôme where Devereux took me and 'Toinette the night I came back. D'you know it?"

"Yes, it's the de Baissac farm."

"I want a hole dug there for tonight. A deep one."

Lemaire nodded and smiled. "About two metres long and one metre wide, eh?"

"Bring back a piece of farm equipment as cover for me."

"OK. I'll be back in time to join in the fun."

"You'll close the garage at six. And the workshops. There'll be nobody there but me and the girl. Maybe not even her. I'll decide that later. Understood?"

Lemaire shrugged. "Why leave it to chance, Chaland. Two can make it easier than one. Why give away any advantage."

"He won't have a chance."

• • •

Once Lemaire had gone Parker plugged in the radio and tapped out his message. The girl had seen him take out the light bulb before he started the transmission, and when it was over she said, "Why did you take out the bulb?"

"Reflex," he said. "It's part of the drill you get used to. If you're transmitting at night and the current is low the light flickers with the morse-key. The Germans notice these things and other people in the house might notice. If there's no light in this room they wouldn't suspect me."

He put a match to the papers and held them over a plate as they burned, and lifted the last corner as the flame enveloped it. He pounded the ashes to a powder with the butt of a knife and went to the toilet and flushed it away. She watched as he put the chair on the table and lifted the radio back up into the loft. Then he tacked the code pad back underneath the table. He turned to look at her.

"Have you got perfume that you use?"

"I don't use perfume."

"I thought you bought some a few weeks back when we were in Brive."

She laughed. "That was for Beauclair to take back in the Lysander for the girls in London."

Parker sighed. "The girls in Baker Street are loaded down with French perfume. They've got so much they use it in their cigarette lighters."

"They won't tell him, Charles," and she was smiling.

"How far is the nearest perfume shop?"

She walked over to the window and pointed.

"There, right opposite."

"Tell me a perfume to ask for."

"Just ask for perfume, Charles. They probably haven't got any. There certainly won't be a choice."

• • •

Parker had drawn the curtains on the office window at Lemaire's garage and left a chink of light showing that was barely visible in the late evening sun. He had sat in the open door of a ramshackle Citröen that was hidden by a lorry and a breakdown truck. The Luger lay heavy in the pocket of his overalls, its butt free of the pocket. He could hear the evening noises from the direction of the town. The gates of the yard were open and his eyes never left them as he waited. He could smell the faint traces of the perfume from where he was hidden and he wondered if he had overdone it.

It was nine-thirty when Nolke came through the big gates and he was carrying a box of chocolates. He walked quite slowly, looking over both sides of the yard as he strolled towards the office. It was dusk now and the light from the window was a thin bar along the concrete.

Nolke paused at the door and listened, his hand poised to knock and his head bent in concentration. His hand hesitated and he moved aside to the window and bent to look through the gap in the curtains. As he stood up the butt of the Luger smashed behind his ear. The box of chocolates fell from his hand as his knees crumpled, and Parker's hands went under his arms, catching him before he fell. He dragged him into the office and the German stirred as his head hit the floor. His eyes opened and Parker could see the glaze on them and then the recognition. Nolke tried to kneel up and Parker's boot caught him at the angle of his throat and jaw. Even as he fought the nausea the German's hand reached inside his jacket for his gun. It fumbled for a moment before his groin exploded in a volcano of red pain. Parker's body straddled the German and his thumbs went up behind Nolke's ear. The German shuddered violently as Parker's body weight came through his thumbs on the pressure point and for a few moments his heels drummed on the floor in reflex, but he had died seconds before.

Parker had lifted the body on to the back of the van and covered it with the sacks of potatoes and the cultivator frame. Lemaire was waiting for him at the farm outside Brantôme and he had wondered in silence why Parker had thrown a box of chocolates in with the corpse. Boxes of chocolates were hard to come by.

They went back to Périgueux together and checked the office at the garage. There was nothing there to connect the place with Nolke. Parker walked back to his room alone, it was too near curfew to go back to Puy Henry.

There was only one bed and he switched out the lights as he and the girl undressed and for the first time he wondered what she looked like naked. And when his body reflexed to his imagination he was glad the room was in black darkness. He arranged his clothes as a pillow for his head and spread his jacket over his body as he stretched out on the floor. As he lay there his mind was on a treadmill of the events of the last two days but as his eyes closed he was aware only of the smell of dust from the threadbare carpet.

• • •

It had seemed only minutes before the knocking on the door, but it was, in fact, almost two hours later and he was standing at the door before he knew what he was doing. The knocking came again. Urgent, almost frantic.

"Who is that?"

"Frenez, let me in Chaland, quickly."

Parker opened the door and Frenez's face was white and strained. The coolness and elegance might never had existed.

"What is it, Frenez?"

Frenez was trembling and Parker led him to a chair by the table. He saw the girl sitting up in bed watching them.

"It's the SS, Chaland. Two hundred of them this morning."

He stopped and looked up at Parker's face as if that were statement enough.

"Go on, André, what happened?"

Frenez was shaking, his whole body racked as if by an ague.

"It was a reprisal for our attack yesterday." He groaned and put his head in his hands and rocked as he wept. Parker put his hands on Frenez's shoulder.

"Tell me, André. Tell me what happened."

The blue eyes looked up at him like a child's and Frenez whispered, "They wiped out Oradour. They came at two o'clock and killed them all. Men, women and children."

"Are you sure?" Parker's voice was dry with shock and disbelief.

"I've been there. They machine-gunned the men in the square. Just mowed them down. They put the women and children in the church and set fire to it and machine-gunned those who tried to get out. There was one survivor. They didn't see him, he came in from the fields and saw it." And he laid his head on the table and sobbed. Parker waited until it was over and Frenez lifted his head. "And they killed the wrong people, my God."

"How?"

"We were at Oradour-sur-Vayres and they wiped out the other Oradour—Oradour-sur-Glane. Somebody told them Oradour and that was it. They went to the wrong Oradour. Six hundred innocent people dead, Chaland, because of what we did. Six hundred and fifty people, 247 schoolchildren. The place is just ruins. The bodies are still there. They won't even let them bury the dead."

Parker was pulling on his trousers as he looked at Frenez. The man was ill. This disaster had been too much even for that tough character. Parker crept down the stairs to the next floor and knocked on the old lady's door. When she opened it on the chain he asked if she would phone for the doctor. He gave her the doctor's name.

It was half an hour before the doctor came but his diagnosis was speedy and decisive. They helped the still distraught man down to the doctor's car. He would phone them from the clinic the next day. He would leave a message with the old lady; she was also a patient of his.

The girl was sitting up in bed as Parker closed the door behind him, and she saw the grim cast of his face. The mouth closed tight and the eyes half-closed. His breathing was shallow and forced, and he leaned back against the door, his arms hanging loose at his sides like a doll's. She pushed aside the thin blanket and swung out her legs and walked over to him. She slid off the dirty jacket, unfastened the belt at his waist and as his trousers fell to his feet she lifted each foot free of the coarse cloth. He walked with her like a child as she led him to the bed. As he lay with his eyes closed she could feel him shivering and her arms went round him. His head cradled against her shoulder, his face against her breasts. She touched his cheek gently and said: "Try to sleep, Charles. Try to sleep." He had shaken his head and through his dry, cracked lips he had said: "I don't think I'll ever sleep again."

"You will, my love," and her hand reached down his body. When it responded she pulled him to her and she lay with her eyes open as he took her. Urgently and fiercely, again and again as if he would never stop. When it was over he lay alongside her and he was almost instantly asleep. All through the night she lay beside him looking at his face, touching his hair. Even asleep, he looked haggard and old, the uneasy life of the past years had been too much and the nightmare of the last two days had been more than even he could take. The self-assurance was beginning to ebb away, and she sensed that he found more comfort from her domesticity than her functions as a courier. The farm cottage at Puy Henry was home and she was mother, sister and companion. Frenez's state of shock had not surprised her but Parker was a different sort of man. Tougher, despite the boyish appearance, and wholly dedicated to what he was doing. When he woke he would wish she had not seen his distress. Wish that he had not had her. Sabine was a hero-worshipper, and as is so often the case she was wrong about her hero on those aspects that touched her personally.

When Parker awoke it was nearly ten o'clock, and the sleep and the new day seemed to have restored his confidence.

She had saved a fresh egg for his breakfast and as they sat together at the small table he seemed to have a need to talk. He had told her about his mother and father, and the house in Birmingham, as if it were something she was entitled to know. And he had told her a little about the leaks from London that so angered him. She realized that he was telling her more than he told the others. And she sensed that their relationship had changed.

He had had to leave at two o'clock to meet Bonnier, but before he left he had arranged for Lemaire to take her back to Puy Henry.

Chapter Nine

Parker had taken the radio back with him to Puy Henry and had arranged with Bonnier for half a dozen of his men to patrol the area of the farm cottage. The small domestic radio was left permanently tuned to the BBC French service.

During the next four weeks there had been nine arms drops and two radio operators had been dropped with radios and spares. 'Toinette was to return on the next Lysander operation, in ten days' time.

Parker had spent two days with Frenez and some of his group leaders. They were concentrating now on destroying locomotives and rolling stock, and Parker had gone with them on the first evening and had showed them how to wire the plastic so that a whole length of track was taken out in a single explosion. The locomotive they had wrecked had been a small 0–6–0 tank engine. They had warned the engine driver and the fireman and they had jumped clear before the track went up and the engine rolled slowly and reluctantly down the embankment in a cloud of white steam. When the boiler exploded it took off half the superstructure and most of the valve gear.

Frenez had settled back into his old role, helped by the fact that not only Oradour but all the other atrocities by the Germans had, in fact, not frightened the population. They were angered and bitter enough to attack the known traitors and collaborators and support the Resistance groups in any way they could. Almost every house was a safe house now.

• • •

'Toinette used the old garage store room for her transmissions. There were rusted gear-boxes and differentials, and oily wooden boxes with rust-encrusted nuts and bolts still locked to sawn-off rods and assemblies. When they were needed they would be valuable stock but as yet they lay unwanted. There were old charts showing tire-pressures for different cars hanging askew on the back of the door, and a calendar for 1940 that had been treasured for the half-naked girl advertising tires.

There was a small but heavy kitchen table which stank of oil and grease with a small metal vice clamped to one edge, and the radio was inside a concealing framework of cardboard boxes with the aerial slung up over one of the angle irons supporting the tin roof. 'Toinette sat at the table to transmit and receive, and one of Lemaire's men always stood outside the window with another at the gates watching for Germans.

She was taking down a long signal from London confirming priority targets, and she had one earpiece of the headphones tucked in her hair so that she could hear a shouted warning and the other she held to her left ear as she scribbled down the coded characters. There were a lot of figures and she guessed they were map references for confirmed special targets but she wouldn't know until she was back in the house decoding. There was no ventilation in the store and sweat had dripped on to her pad. She wiped her mouth with the back of her hand and went on working. Ten minutes later the transmission closed and London signed off with the code-word and 'Toinette Cousteau pulled off the headphones from the tangle of her hair and leaned back in her chair. It was the last normal thing she would ever do. As always she looked through the window to see which of Lemaire's men would help her put away the radio. The man who was looking through the window was a stranger. And he was pointing a Luger at her. And as she stood up the gun jabbed at the glass and the window pane shattered. She stood quite still as the man withdrew the pistol and put in his hand to lift the latch and swung the window open.

"Don't move, Mam'selle. Just stay quite still." And as he walked round the shack to the door she raced for the window and her knee was on the sill when his hand grabbed her hair and she fell back screaming.

The German stood looking down at her as she sprawled on the floor and he turned briefly as another man came through the door. Despite the summer heat he was wearing the typical Gestapo give-away, a long black leather overcoat. He stood alongside the man with the gun and looked down at her. He looked at her face and then at a paper he held in his hand. He turned to the man with the gun.

"This is her, Gunther. Let's take her back."

He reached down and grabbed the neck of her blouse and jerked her to her feet.

As they took her through the garage she saw Lemaire and four of his men. They were manacled and there was blood on their faces and clothes. Nobody moved or spoke as they led her past the little group. She stumbled as they roughly pushed her ahead of them to the black car that was parked in the yard. She was shoved into the back seat with the Gestapo men on each side of her. As the doors swung to, the driver let in the clutch and the car moved off quickly. They passed through the centre of Périgueux, and as they left the town area she knew they were taking her to the Gestapo house in the wealthy suburb on the far side of the bridge over the river on the road that led to Cahors.

The big iron gates were open as they swung into the driveway and the car followed the circular path to pull up in front of the big house. The poplars cast long shadows across the lawns as the sun went down behind the low hills. It was a perfect summer evening for the people of Périgord and the white doves that circled the "pigeonnier" by the stables alongside the house.

The hallway was empty except for a big switchboard and two operators. And the two men took the girl up the wide curving stairway to the first floor. The former bedrooms were offices. Bare and stark with desks and a chair or two. They pushed her to the farthest room and the hand-painted lettering on the door said "Gunther Heine." The man with the gun pushed her inside and waved her to the chair by the desk. The other man said something in German, laughed, and walked away, taking off his leather coat. The man she assumed was Heine sat down at the desk and pulled out a slide and lay the Luger on it. Then he leaned back and looked at the girl.

"What's your name?"

"Cousteau. Antoinette Cousteau."

"Where do you live?"

"At the garage."

"There's no living accommodation at the garage. Where do you live?"

His teeth rasped slowly over his bottom lip as he looked at her silently. Then he turned to look out of the window. After a few moments he turned back to her.

"Let me tell you mam'selle that we know all about your group and the man whose code-name is Georges, who came by Lysander from London. There's no need for you to suffer. All we want is to tidy up a few details."

The girl was silent. She had noted the mistake about the plane.

"It's stupid, my dear, to play the heroine. It's a lovely summer evening. You should be out with some young man, not sitting here. These people don't care about you, you know. You've been arrested, so they'll replace you, and they'll commit more stupidities and the innocent population will suffer. They run around France like schoolboys. What do they achieve? The armies will decide the war not these cowboys playing games."

He pulled out a drawer and pushed across a packet of Gauloises.

"Have a cigarette."

"I don't smoke."

He smiled. "You do, my dear. Just look at the nicotine on your right-hand fingers."

He stood up and walked round the desk to stand in front of her.

"What times are your radio schedules?"

She shook her head.

"What does that mean?"

She looked up at him: "I am an officer in the British Army. I will only give you my name, rank and number."

His harsh laugh startled her. "My dear young woman, you are in civilian clothes, you were caught working an illegal radio transmitter—you are a spy and we are entitled to treat you as such unless you co-operate, and I'm afraid that won't be very nice for you." He turned sharply and walked back to her and roughly lifted her chin so that she had to look at him.

"You're a very pretty girl, my dear, and they would be very enthusiastic. You know what I mean?"

She spat and the small pool of saliva went no further than the back of his hand. He pulled out a handkerchief and wiped his hand slowly as he looked at her. Then he walked to the door and called out in German. An elderly corporal with a submachine-gun came in and the officer gave him some order in German. Then he turned to the girl.

"I shall leave you for five minutes to reflect on your position. The guard has orders to shoot you if you attempt to escape."

And the door closed behind him.

• • •

The corporal had watched her, gun pointing, until Heine came back. He had left her for half an hour on the chance that she would recognize in the time the hopelessness of her situation.

He was smoking a thin cigar as he stood in front of her, looking at her face.

"Well, my dear, what is it to be, a sensible discussion in private between you and me or . . ." and he put out both hands as if he could not bear to name the alternative.

The girl said nothing but he could see that she was trembling.

"It will be your responsibility, mam'selle. Not mine. The choicc is entirely yours."

He watched her face as he drew on his cigar, inhaled deeply, and then slowly blew out the smoke. He walked over to his desk and pressed a bell. She could hear it ringing far across the building. There was the clatter of boots along the landing and an officer in SS uniform came in with four SS men. Heine had waved to the girl and he said in French "Persuade her." And he had turned at the door and said to the girl, "I'll see you in half an hour." And the door had closed.

The SS officer was a big man, his hair cut short almost to his scalp. There were heavy pock-marks on his cheeks and neck and he stood with hands on his hips as if he were a wrestler starting a bout. He stood in front of the girl and said in bad French, "What time you go on air, fräulein?"

She made no answer and when his open hand was lifted she flinched and bowed her head. When no blow landed she lifted her head and that was when he struck her. It was with his open hand but the pain was unexpected and the shock of what was happening was intense. She remembered what they had said when she was training—"Hold out for forty-eight hours to let the others disperse and then talk as little as you have to. Be unconscious as soon as you can. That uses up time."

His hand roughly lifted her chin so that she was forced to look at him.

"One more chance, fräulein. Only one."

His thumb pressed into her chin as he held her and she closed her eyes, and she hunched her shoulders to take the blow.

But his hand was at the collar of her blouse and it pulled sharply. Buttons bounced on the floor but somehow the seams held until the man's free hand held her shoulders as his other hand wrenched and tore at her clothes. The blouse hung in tatters and she fell backwards off the chair as he loosened the leather belt of her skirt. She felt the thin cloth stretch and tear and the ceiling slid and turned as his fingers dug deep in her long hair and pulled her to her feet. He hooked up the chair with his foot and she could smell his stale breath as his hand reached for her brassiere and wrenched it from her breasts. His hand grabbed the thin strip of her panties across her hips and with two sharp tugs it was broken. His hand closed round her wrist and as she struggled his other fist smashed in a blinding crashing explosion on her nose. Then his hands went on her breasts, her feet off the floor as he flung her on the desk. The edge caught her spine a sickening blow and then he was on her, his body thrusting into hers. They took turns having her and she was faintly conscious of voices raised in anger before she lost consciousness.

Heine had stood watching the girl come back to consciousness. She was still naked, her hands handcuffed behind her, her arms over the back of the chair. There was blood caked on her mouth and breasts from her broken nose, and blood still trickled from her swollen lips. There was vomit on her thighs and between her legs, and lacerations on her breasts and shoulders.

As Heine watched, the girl lifted her head. One eye was completely closed and she turned her sound eye away from the light of the window and saw Heine. She looked down at her nakedness and remembered what had happened.

"Are you going to co-operate now, Mam'selle?"

The girl didn't answer.

"The boys are still enthusiastic, my dear. It's them or me."

She lifted her blood-caked face: "When it's all over it will be your turn. We shall not forget. The others will still find you wherever you are."

Heine pulled up another chair and sat in front of her.

"Do you really believe that, my dear. The Allies have bitten off more than they can chew. They've come to a halt in Normandy and that's as far as they'll get. We shall throw them back into the Channel and then it will be their turn." He paused for a few moments and then went on, "I am not asking you to betray your friends, just the times of your schedules and your security check words. Nobody will ever know."

A vision of the gardens at Wanborough came into her mind. Trees and lawns and geraniums in pots, and the man had said: "If you talk at all, you'll go on talking. So you don't talk. Don't try and be clever with lies. They'll break you down. Just don't talk. Name, rank and number and quote the Geneva Convention." Heine's slow soft voice made her want to sleep.

"When we've had a chat you can be released. I give you my word of honour."

She slowly lifted her head.

"Is all this," and she nodded at her body, "part of your honour? Is this what the Geneva Convention says?"

"My dear, that's for prisoners-of-war. No court anywhere would consider you as in that category. Civilian clothes, forged documents, a British-made transmitter. You're a spy, my dear, an enemy agent. The people who sent you here must have warned you that you are outside the law, outside any convention."

He waited patiently for a response and when it didn't come he said: "I really can't wait much longer, Antoinette. I shall have to call them back again."

And when he said her name she felt the sting of her tears on the raw flesh of her mouth. She wanted to wipe out the nightmare. She had packed up her radio and Lemaire had put it in his hiding place in the inspection pit. She had gone back to the house next door and they had had their meal and walked in the fields looking for mushrooms, the dog racing through the high grass, long ears flapping as he searched for rabbits.

Heine's hand lifted her head roughly by her hair and she could see the anger on his face.

"Maybe you liked it mam'selle. They tell us that the French girls are experienced in these things."

Her teeth clamped on his hand and she felt them grate on his bones as he snatched his hand away.

She was alone for a few moments and then the black-shirted hooligans were back. She saw the anticipation on their faces and their silence was purposeful. One of them cursed in French as her handcuffs caught in the struts of the chair and she was jerked upright by her hair and hands grabbed at her body as they hustled her again to the desk. A hand held her head down with her hair, and other hands roughly pulled her legs apart as the first man took her. The pain was as if her body was tearing and as the waves of nausea flowed over her she felt her bowels void and a voice shouted, "The filthy bitch," and the ceiling seemed to float away as she lost consciousness.

• • •

Parker had been with Bonnier in the hills at St. Jean-de-Cole when Sabine brought the news of 'Toinette's capture.

He had gone straight back to Périgueux to find Devereux. Already the reseau had moved houses and meeting places. They met together late in the afternoon in the vestry at the cathedral. One of Devereux's men stood guard at the door.

"What do they know, Jean-Luc, and who betrayed the girl?"

"I don't think they know anything beyond the set-up at the garage."

"Did they get the radio?"

"Yes, and the code pads and the messages she had taken down from London."

"When did they take her?"

"Yesterday, yesterday evening."

"Where is she?"

"We're not sure. She's not in the prison. She's not at the SD place or the Gestapo office in Périgueux. She's probably in the Gestapo house over the river."

"And Lemaire and his men?"

"The Germans shot them at the prison this morning."

"And who betrayed them?"

Devereux sighed. "The girl's lover. They had quarrelled."

"Go on."

"She wanted to leave him. She preferred one of Lemaire's men."

"That's a reason. Where's the proof?"

Devereux shrugged. "You know that proof is not possible, Chaland. Since the arrests the man has had a nervous breakdown. He's receiving treatment in hospital."

"Which hospital?"

"The German army field-hospital at Ribérac."

For a moment Parker closed his eyes. When he opened them he said, "Is he under guard?"

"There's no special guard for him. The camp itself is guarded."

"Contact Bonnier. I want him to raid the place tomorrow. Send a man who knows the traitor well. I want him killed."

There was knocking at the vestry door. The guard peered in. "There's a messenger for you, chief," and he looked towards Devereux.

"Send him in."

The young boy carried an envelope and stood while Devereux read it. "You can go," he said to the boy, and he handed the paper to Parker.

It just said: "Mademoiselle Cousteau died at noon today. Her corpse despatched by train to Paris address Rue des Saussies, Paris, Marie-Claire."

Parker handed back the note in silence. The address was one of the Gestapo offices in Paris. Then he said quietly, "Who is Marie-Claire?"

"A nurse at the hospital. We have many contacts there."

"Find out how she died so that I can tell London."

• • •

Sabine was out when he got back to the room in Périgueux and the place seemed too empty, too quiet, too still. There were things to be done and he didn't do them. He walked across to the window and looked out at the street. He wondered which direction she would come from. He missed her.

He leaned against the drab velvet curtains, his head resting against the window frame. He thought of 'Toinette and the car trip they had made from Beaulieu to Winchester. He remembered seeing her crouched in a small circle on the lawn around an instructor, her fingers connecting and strapping the detonators to some "plastique," the brown eyes looking up for approval. And sometimes he had walked with her to the place where she was billeted, the house called Rings, and he had tested her morse with dih-dah-dih-dah's as they had walked. And she had talked of her English mother who made dresses for middle-class ladies in Tunbridge Wells. Sometimes she had knocked on his cottage door in the early hours of the morning, looking beautiful and excited from an evening at some night-club in London. She would sit on his bed and tell him about the young men who tried to pick her up. There was a Free French "capitaine" who featured from time to time in the saga, and he wondered if he would care that the pretty girl was dead. And for the first time since he had joined SOE he wondered if what the girl had been doing was valuable enough to the war effort to equate with what would have been a degrading death. The schoolmaster lover who loved her and betrayed her was already as good as dead, but Parker's mind slid away from an attempt at justification. Surely when it was all over there would be a reckoning. The Germans would be brought to justice for their crimes against the Resistance and the fighters would be remembered and rewarded. But he had had no explanation from London as to how a German Gestapo man in Limoges could know about the structure of SOE in England and the code-name of his own operation. Or could the traitor be one of his own people in the field?

He fetched down the radio and tuned it to the BBC. He turned the volume down low so that he would hear the girl's footsteps. It was the third message and it had almost passed before he recognized that it was his release message for the special operation. The next radio transmission from London would be for him alone. The special operation. The next transmission was at midnight Greenwich Mean Time. He half listened to the other messages and the bulletins. More advances had been made in Normandy and there were rumours, the BBC reported, that General Tojo had resigned in Japan.

Parker grew more agitated as the evening wore on and the girl had not returned. He was angry and depressed. His anger had disappeared when she arrived pale-faced and dishevelled just after ten. There was a bruise on her cheek and blood on her mouth.

"What happened, Sabine?"

"I went to Puy Henry."

"But why?"

There were tears in her eyes. "I was foolish, Charles. That cottage is a home for me. I first saw you there. I wanted a little peace, and there was food wasting there."

"So what happened?"

"The Gestapo were inside. Waiting."

"Go on."

"They checked my papers and I said I had nothing to do with the cottage. I was walking on the hill and I was curious. I said I was staying with Monsieur le Comte."

"So why the bruises on your mouth?"

"One of the men tried to have sex with me in the barn. I shouted and screamed and a Gestapo officer came. I told him I was pregnant and he took me back to the cottage."

"He could have called a doctor to check if he suspected you. Positive grounds for arrest on suspicion."

The white face looked young and defenceless and the soft mouth quivered. "I *am* pregnant, Charles. The doctor told me yesterday. *He* will be certain in ten days' time. *I* am certain now."

She saw the astonishment on his face. This was going to be one more load on his back and she wondered what his reaction would be.

He reached for the chair and sat down looking up at her face. And her heart melted as he smiled and said the lines of Malherbe's old poem:

> "Ce sera vous qui de nos villes
> Ferez la beauté refleurir,
> Vous, qui de nos haines civiles
> Ferez la racine mourir;
> Et par vous la paix assurée
> N'aura pas la courte durée
> Qu'espèrent infidèlement,
> Non lasses de notre souffrance . . ."

And smiling she took up the words,

> "Ces Français qui n'ont de la France
> Que la langue et l'habillement."

He held out his arms and she clung to him with her head on his shoulder and he gently stroked her pliant back. He looked up at her face, smiling. "We'll ask the good Catholic Lemaire to find a priest to marry us, my love."

She stroked his face, "Lemaire is dead, Charles."

For a moment he closed his eyes: "Devereux will find us one."

They had eaten and he had made love to her, gently and tenderly. And she felt part of summer, part of her normal world and she thought of the lines of the poem again. She would make the beauty of the town flower for him again, this Englishman who was more French than many Frenchmen. And for the first time for months Parker had slept soundly, unmoving beside the girl.

• • •

It was Devereux's knocking at the door that awoke them the following morning. The Germans had arrived at the cottage at Puy Henry and had fired the barns of hay and straw before arresting the farmer and his wife.

The SS division was preparing to go north as reinforcements and were pillaging and raping over a wide area. He had heard that a senior Communist had come down from Paris to confer with Bonnier. There was talk of French army officers representing de Gaulle who were giving orders to the Resistance groups.

Devereux stopped the litany of woe as Parker held up his hand. "Jean-Luc. Sabine and I are going to be married. Can you find us a priest who will co-operate?"

• • •

Laws, statutes and regulations had been pushed aside and Devereux's men had mounted guard inside and outside the small church at Chateau-l'Eveque as the priest performed the ceremony. The old Comte and his wife and Devereux himself had been the only witnesses. The organist had weaved a strand of the "Marseillaise" into the softly played psalm as the priest signed the documents. And down the path to the lych-gate Devereux's men had laid out "la jouchée," the traditional bridal path of moss and flowers. They had all gone back, a quiet, happy group, to the room in Périgueux.

The Comte had produced his miracle of champagne and they had toasted the groom and his bride. Then the Comte and his wife had left with the farm van and only Devereux had stayed. He had been giving Devereux new orders when he remembered. He had missed the midnight transmission that would give him the special operational orders. He brought the transmitter down from the loft and tapped out a request for a repeat transmission. It was an hour before they came back to him and the message was quite short. But it took ten minutes to decode and when he had read it he passed it across the table to Devereux. It read:

> "Figures 9704 stop To LANTERN stop Operation Ratweek stop All groups authorized herewith to eliminate all local personnel of Abwehr, Sicherheitsdienst and Gestapo stop message ends acknowledge."

Devereux shrugged. "Maybe those boys are waking up at last."

"How many men have you got to spare, Jean-Luc? Tough ones."

"Three, maybe four."

"That's not enough."

"How many do you need?"

"At least twelve, apart from you and me." He stood up. "Send a messenger up to Bonnier and tell him what I want. He had better come too."

"And if his Commie friends object?"

"Then tell Bonnier there will be no more drops. Moscow can send their supplies."

Devereux had nodded and left.

• • •

Parker had walked with the girl down to the bank of the river. They sat on the shallow slope. The river was glassy and slow-moving, blue from the sky with reflections of the tall mace and yellow irises that flanked its edges. Kingfishers darted and swooped and fish rose to make silent circles on the smooth surface of the water. He laced his fingers in hers and turned to look at her. "I thought I was so observant but I never saw how beautiful you are. I was stupid."

"You'll never be stupid, my love. You had work to do. Too many other things to occupy your mind."

"I think we should find a small cottage near Brantôme."

"Are you sure you want to stay in France? What about England?"

He shrugged. "There's nothing there for me. I belong here. We'll go to see my mother's grave and I'll show you where we lived."

"And what will you do?"

He smiled. "I'll do what I'm supposed to be doing now. Repair farm machinery. There's going to be money in farming when it's over."

"How long will that be?"

"Two months. Maybe three. Not long, my love."

He put his arm round her tightly. "What do you want, a boy or a girl?"

"We'll have a boy first and then a girl."

There was a breeze now across the river, bending the rushes and brushing the surface with quivering patches that shimmered in the fading light. For Parker it was a new world. A world in which, like other men, he had a stake. A wife, and a child to be born. They would have a cottage and they would walk to meet him from his work. And those two would be his to care for. An easy, light load compared to what he now had. It was like being unlocked, set free, born again.

They walked back slowly through the town. It was not yet free of Germans but there were smiles on the French people's faces, and here and there some bold spirit had hung out a tricolour. It was the 24th of August and, although they didn't know it, Leclerc's armoured division was thrusting into Paris and the streets crackled with small-arms fire as the

Germans surrendered the capital. Parker was too occupied that evening to hear the BBC news. He had kissed the girl goodbye and told her to sleep because he would not be back until mid-morning the following day. She had laughed softly with pleasure as he laid his head like a baby's on her shoulder while she stroked his neck.

• • •

They sat round the long dining-table at the back of the inn. There were three cars, two trucks and two motorcycles parked at the edge of the orchard behind the inn. The table was covered with large-scale maps which Devereux had long ago "borrowed" from the Town Hall.

Only Bonnier, Devereux and Parker sat at the table. The others were posted around the inn and checking the weapons and ammunition in the stables. Parker sensed the tension between himself and Bonnier. He was only chief in name now. Bonnier questioned London's motives and talked of referring the operation to Paris. Bonnier was there despite his Moscow orders, and the old comradeship that brought him there was a loyalty to Parker and Devereux, not to London or SOE. All of them sensed that there were only weeks now before the Germans were thrown out of France, and there were other things to be won now. Votes, power, and a battle for people's minds. Parker was the only man in the three reseaux whose mind was still concerned only with the Resistance.

Bonnier was pointing at one of the maps, looking up at Parker as he spoke.

"I'd like to have those boys if you've no objection." His thick finger was pointing at the Gestapo HQ. It was an ideal target for Bonnier and his men, but Devereux and Parker suspected that the Communist was looking for the applause that came from attacking the best known of the three German counter-intelligence organizations. To the local people all German Intelligence was the Gestapo.

Parker shrugged. "How many men will you need?"

"A driver and eight men."

"There are only fifteen of us all told. And there are four targets."

"Four?"

"There's the Gestapo mansion outside the town, across the river."

Bonnier smiled grimly up at Parker. "The place they took that stupid bitch of a radio operator."

"She's dead, Bonnier."

"I know, my friend. I had two men killed finishing off the traitor in the hospital. Remember?"

"You take four men, Bonnier." He turned to look at Devereux. "You take four men too, Jean-Luc. I'll take the others to cover the Abwehr people and the Gestapo place outside town."

Parker turned back to look at Bonnier. "The first thing you do at Gestapo HQ is cut the telephone wires. I don't want them to warn the men at the big house."

They shared out the vehicles and the weapons, and Parker took the men who Bonnier and Devereux had left behind. They had synchronized their watches and assembled their own groups in separate rooms.

Bonnier and his men had left just before midnight and Devereux had left at ten minutes past midnight. Theirs was the nearest target.

There was nothing on the road. No people. No vehicles. The curfew was still the law, but even the usual German troops and Feldgendarmerie were not on the streets.

The elegant Abwehr house stood back from the road, its white-painted front lit by the moon. There were lights downstairs and on the first floor. There were two Wehrmacht privates guarding the open gates. The one who was smoking had reached for his rifle propped up against the wooden box as the knife went into him just once, and the rough hand covered his mouth and nose. As his companion whirled to see what was happening the pick handle lashed at his head and he moaned as he hit the ground. Parker rolled him over and shone the torch on his eyes. He was safely dead.

The gravel crunched under their feet as they ran to the front door. It wasn't locked and Parker was the first man in. He flung open the door on the right as the others went past him. The room was empty although the light was burning. As he ran across the hall the other door opened and Parker pumped five shots into the man who was walking out. As he burst into the room a man in civilian clothes was rising from the chair at his desk. His eyes bulged with fright and he was putting up his hands as the bullets laced from his lower ribs in a diagonal to his left shoulder. The noise of the shooting seemed to go on echoing round the otherwise silent house.

The others were cutting phone leads and smashing the communications radios. He called them to him and they ran back to the vehicles.

• • •

It was twenty minutes later before they were at the house across the river. Devereux's man was waiting for them.

There were two Gestapo officers, four sergeants and three civilian clerks on the premises and he had found a servant of the previous owners in the village who had sketched out a rough layout of the house. An officer, a sergeant and a clerk were on duty on the ground floor.

A big Wehrmacht truck had been driven in fifteen minutes earlier and had crossed the quadrangle by the stables. No telephone wires had been cut as yet, so that the Germans would not be given any prior warning by dead lines.

The house was set well back from the road. It was built of a light sandstone and was about 200 years old. The big front door was framed by an old fig tree that was beginning to run wild. On each wing of the house there was a six-windowed bay, and lights from the windows shone yellow across the drive and the lawns. The wide entrance to the driveway was open, with wrought iron gates fixed back by blocks of stone.

Parker took two men with him over the wall, leaving Devereux and the others to follow as soon as they heard firing in the house. There was a tall hedge about half-way across the lawns and Parker crawled there with his men. They lay watching the big entrance door. It was half open and light flowed down the wide stone steps and they could hear music from a radio. He was to go in first and the other two would give him covering fire. He wanted to get up to the first floor if possible before he opened fire.

They crawled slowly across the lawns and ran crouching

across the gravel driveway and Parker stood flattened against the stone frame of the door as he slowly moved his head to look inside the hall. A civilian sat at a field telephone-exchange in the middle of the hall, reading a book and smoking. Parker pointed silently and the others understood and nodded. He grinned as he reached out and they handed him the sock with wet sand.

As he stood inside the entrance the radio was loud enough to drown any slight sound he might make and he walked firmly and surely to the back of the man at the telephone board. The heavy sock took him behind the ear and Parker caught him before he fell. He laid the inert body on the floor and raced silently up the broad staircase. His eye caught the writing on a card pinned across one of the doors. It said "Obersturmbannführer Keitel" and he headed straight for it.

He had made two strides when he heard the shouts and the clattering of boots and as he turned he saw that the hall was full of Germans in field grey, and as he went to turn and head again for the office door a strong arm crooked across his throat and as his head went back something metallic struck his hand and the Tommy-gun hit his leg as it clattered to the tiled floor. A pistol dug into his spine and another ground into his ear. His arms were thrust behind his back and handcuffs snapped so tight that a fold of his skin was caught in the ratchet. The arm left his throat and as he was released he saw a tall man, elegant in his SS uniform, standing watching him, smoking a cigarette in a long holder. His lean handsome face showed no emotion and his pale grey eyes watched without blinking. He waved with his cigarette towards the open office and Parker was hustled inside and thrown clumsily on to the chair. The officer walked in slowly and sat on the edge of the desk, one long leg swinging easily as he looked at Parker without speaking. Then, looking at his cigarette holder as he inserted a fresh cigarette, he said without looking up:

"Well, m'sieur, you really are in trouble." He looked up at Parker as he lit his cigarette. When he got no answer he broke the match and searched for a place to put the remains. He threw them towards the fireplace.

"We caught your Communist friend at long last, Monsieur Chaland. I must tell you that five Gestapo officers were killed and that means execution for you and Bonnier. Your people left our transmitter on and we heard the performance. We were waiting for you, Chaland." He smiled a sour half smile. "You know you can't take on the Gestapo *and* the German Army, my friend." He stood up. "But I'm glad you tried, we've wanted you for a long time."

He walked over to stand in front of Parker.

"The little gang in Orchard House will miss you too. Especially Foster and Fredericks. You must have been their model pupil. You were in too much of a hurry tonight, Chaland. What was it the chaps at Wanborough Manor always used to tell you boys—"Time spent in reconnaissance is seldom wasted." They were right you know, Chaland. What was all the hurry tonight?"

Parker looked up at the handsome face. "Are you Keitel?"

The man nodded and Parker went on. "There's no need for us to play games, Keitel. I'll give you name, rank and number. Nothing else. Just call your thugs."

Keitel held up his hands. "Not so much hurry, my hero. Remember we've got Bonnier too." He wheeled round suddenly, pointing at Parker. "Where's your radio?"

And before Parker could have spoken the door burst open and two men stood holding up Bonnier. His eyes were closed and his head lolled sideways. Blood covered his face. Hideously bright red. Keitel shouted, "Take him away, you bloody fools, take him away." He stamped his foot and his pale face was reddening with anger. "For Christ's sake," he said to no one in particular.

Again he stood in front of Parker. "Are you sure you want the rough stuff, my friend? It seems a pity. You'll talk in the end. They always do." He waved his cigarette in a wide arc. "We have three SOE men working for us you know, and two women. There's very little you can tell us that we don't know."

Parker lifted his eyebrows. "Why bother with me then?"

Keitel pulled over another chair and sat astride it facing Parker, his elbows resting on the back of the chair. The cold eyes looked over Parker's face: "Do your people really want the Bolsheviks to take over in France?"

Parker smiled. "We don't care as long as they are Frenchmen not Germans."

"For God's sake, Chaland, Bolsheviks are under orders from Moscow. They want to take over the world. And we want to stop them."

"And I want the Germans out of France."

Keitel stood up and sighed. "My God, my God, what times we live in." And he walked to the door and left it open behind him.

• • •

Three hours later he had come to. He was naked and shivering and the red weals were wet with pus and his body felt as if it was on fire. He could smell burnt hair but his arms were too heavy with pain to move to find what hair was burnt. He tried to move his head but it wouldn't respond. A shadow came across his face and he saw Keitel looking at him. He heard Keitel order somebody to fetch the doctor and a few minutes later he heard Keitel say, "For Christ's sake, how can he talk with a dislocated jaw. Fix it. Quickly."

Inside his head he heard the bones grating as the doctor hooked back his jaw. He felt the sweat burst out of him with the pain. Then it was Keitel's face again.

"Chaland, can you hear me?"

Parker made no answer and he closed his eyes.

"Chaland, I know about the girl. The girl named Sabine. I'm checking the church records now for her address."

Parker's eyes opened and there was nothing he could do to stop the tears that slowly ran scalding down his face.

• • •

Later the same day General de Gaulle entered Paris. In Warsaw the Poles rose against their German oppressors and the Russians halted their troops the other side of the Vistula and waited until the rising had been ruthlessly crushed by the Germans. The people who organized such risings could do the same again some day against their new masters. It was better if their deaths were chalked up to the Germans. And the same day the Russians entered Bucharest.

• • •

The following month SOE operations in France were wound up by London with what some said was indecent haste. There were extraordinarily few medals, the British authorities seemed to find few heroes or heroines. And General de Gaulle refused to shake hands with British officers of the Resistance. Dozens of agents were unaccounted for, slaughtered without dignity or honour in one concentration camp or another. Young women shackled like animals spent their last hours in filthy huts and cells. In the world outside the Germans were fighting their last battles while their SS compatriots did their best to eliminate the victims who could testify to their crimes. Four SOE girls in Natzweiler camp were given shots of phenol and then cremated alive. The slaughter went on against the holocaust outside.

Next of kin received encouraging news from Baker Street concerning agents who were long since dead.

Sabine Chaland *née* Patou had been given two widow's pensions. One from the British and one from the French. And eighteen months later she had stood in the rain while an officer from Paris had pinned the posthumous Croix de Guerre on to the black dress that she wore along with the others. The name of Charles Chaland was carved with the other names on the glassy, pink stone plaque on the north side of the war memorial in Périgueux. The south side was already full of names from World War I.

The baby was a girl and she had been baptized Chantal Marie. For almost five years several decent men who knew her background had made their tentative advances regarding marriage or bed towards the pretty widow. After that time they had given up and newcomers to the area found more amenable ladies.

When the little girl was three they had moved to a house in Brantôme to be nearer the school and those who didn't know, wondered why the young widow so frequently toiled up the steep hill at Puy Henry, to sit while the small girl picked wild flowers in the summer, or stood in winter winds with her dark straight hair blowing across her cold rosy cheeks.

When the little girl was six it had been she who wore her father's medal as they stood at the war memorial for the annual ceremony. And when she grew up she remembered fondly what her mother had so often said, "Et ton père disait toujours. . . ."

PART THREE

Chapter Ten

Bailey stopped the MG on the south side of Battersea Bridge. The top was down and it was just beginning to rain. That wasn't why he had stopped, but he got slowly out of the car and put it up as he tried to focus something in his mind's eye. He could see a picture, a photograph, and there was something wrong. Where the hell had it been? In a newspaper somewhere. The rain was coming down fast and his shirt was soaked. He slid back into the seat and moved off slowly towards Sloane Square.

He was shaving when the memory flooded back. It was six months ago when he had seen the picture. It was one of the press cuttings in Walters's flat. There were soldiers at the war memorial, he had assumed that they were English, but he realized now that their helmets were French; there was a ridge down the centre. And the immigration stamps on the passport were for entry to France, and the song was "J'ai deux amours." And he'd been seen by the MI6 man at an art gallery in Paris a couple of weeks before he died. And he had forgotten to check the birth certificate.

He had picked up the girl and they had eaten at Leoni's

Quo Vadis, and after he had dropped her at her flat he drove back to New Scotland Yard, a happy mixture of self-righteousness for not having chatted the girl into bed, and anticipation of what he might find. It would not be possible to check the birth certificate until the following morning.

Bailey wasn't an efficient bachelor and that was why he had chosen the two-room flat. His cooking leaned towards tins and fish-fingers, the décor was accidental, but the furniture was comfortable. The single bed was typical of the man. Given the prerequisites of lust or affection two bodies could easily be accommodated, and frequently were. But its formal singularity spoke of ascetic bachelorhood, and, Bailey reasoned, would avoid questions from the small boy. On another level he was equally aware that small boys see no significance in the width of beds. But it was a tribute, a proof of something or other. He knew that by instinct.

He looked along the bookshelves for something to take his mind off his thoughts about Walters, and took down the still unread *Decline and Fall* and Thomson's *Europe since Napoleon* and put them on the low table beside his chair. He sipped slowly and absent-mindedly at the glass of claret. In his job, he thought, he had succeeded because of his clarity of thought. Why, he wondered, could he not have the same clarity in his personal relationships. Why was it always so confused and uncertain.

Like many others who succeeded in the business of intelligence or counter-intelligence, Bailey had never been entirely accurate in assessing his own skills. His P file would have given him the clues. Even in his work it was not logical analysis that made him successful, it was imagination. The logic was generally rationalization and often fallacious. The university degree made him apply reason where reason seldom lay. And if you spend most of your life analysing other people's characters and motivations with cynicism and suspicion you are likely to abandon that attitude in your private life. And in his private life Bailey abandoned his training. Brown eyes were loving, and blue eyes were frank and truthful. And girls were defenceless.

As he read Thomson on "the system of Metternich" the thoughts about Walters seeped through. Maybe *he* was like

Walters. They were both holed up in their small sanctuaries. Half-hidden from the rest of the world. What would the people in the downstairs flat say of *him,* if they were asked. He stood up and looked around the room. Thank God, he thought, for the books.

• • •

He waited impatiently for the brown envelope to come up. He had the feeling that maybe he had found a corner of the jig-saw puzzle.

He emptied the newspaper cuttings on to his desk and sorted through to find the picture. It was brown at the edges and the main area was yellow with age. He walked down the corridor to the laboratory and put it under a low-powered microscope. The assistant came over and watched him trying to adjust the focusing knob.

"It won't help you, Commander. You'll just break the screen into individual dots. Try this glass over here."

The assistant laid the photograph under a plastic lens and slowly adjusted the height of the frame. Then he stood aside. "That's the most you'll get without break-up."

He looked through the flat lens. There were twenty or so men in civilian clothes but wearing decorations—and in the centre a woman holding the hand of a small girl who had a medal pinned to her blouse. Four soldiers had rifles at the present, and a bugler had his bugle to his lips. The monument itself was on the right-hand side of the picture and the editorial cropping had cut off most of the flag that filled the top left corner. It was quite impossible to make out the identity of anybody in the picture.

He slid the cutting from under the lens and turned it over. The text was in French and there were snippets about the harvest, a new bridge, and market prices for vegetables and fruit at Périgueux. He looked at the assistant: "Is it possible to get an enlargement of the magnified picture?"

"Oh, yes, we can photograph the cutting and blow it up to any size image you want."

"By tomorrow mid-day?"

"Sure. How many copies?"

"Half a dozen."

"Will 10 x 8s do?"

"That'd be fine."

He left the cutting with the assistant and went back to his own office.

He sat and collected the cuttings of the classified advertisements. They were all roughly two inches long and one newspaper column wide. There were nine of them and he laid them side by side, their top edges level with each other. Then he read the top of each cutting. Some were box numbers, some private addresses, and some were business addresses.

There was second-hand furniture for sale, offers for landscape gardening, musical instruments, second mortgages, loans up to £5,000 without security, tax advice, and a number of household services. Some advertisements only appeared once and others were repeated in every issue. There were no personal messages. He turned the cuttings over and checked the news items on the reverse side and started putting them in date order. The latest was ten months old and the earliest two years earlier, most of the others were unidentifiable. He turned them face upwards again and saw it straight away. A two line advertisement that just said "French polishing by skilled men 01–059 6048." The same advertisement appeared on every cutting but each time the telephone number was different. He wrote out of list of the numbers for the proper authorities to check for him. Then he drove home and slept.

• • •

Chief Superintendent Murphy pressed his thumb against his nose as if it might aid his thinking. Bailey sat waiting for a response. Finally Murphy reached for the phone and asked for Paynter. He waited, listened and then said, "Contact him there and get him to phone me on a scrambler."

He turned to Bailey. "He's at Portsmouth. They'll get him. Are they still using these phone numbers?"

"Only the Hungarian one."

The phone rang and Murphy put the receiver to his ear and pressed the scrambler button.

"Thanks for calling back, Paynter. D'you remember the case of the man Walters. The one who killed himself . . . yes, that's the one . . . your chap saw him at the embassy and an SIS man saw him in Paris . . . no we didn't close the file at FO request through Lovegrove. . . . Commander Bailey was on it and he's unearthed a bit more . . . there's a separate lead back to France, nothing exciting but it looks like he *was* in contact with our friends . . . what . . . he had some telephone numbers . . . two at the Soviet embassy, two of Polish embassy staff and the Hungarian press attaché's private number . . . what do you think, d'you want him to follow up? . . . I think so . . . fine, fine, leave it with me. Cheers."

Murphy hung up and looked across at Bailey.

"Much as I expected. Agrees that you should take the enquiry a bit further. We can't ignore those bloody telephone numbers.

"Can I use all facilities?"

"Of course."

• • •

Bailey looked slowly over the entries on the birth certificate. He had got the impression from the Palmers that Walters had no relatives, and from the birth certificate all he had got was details of the place of birth. A street in South Croydon. He walked up Kings Road to the garage and checked out his car and headed for Chelsea Bridge. It was a Friday night and the traffic was heavy with workers going home and people heading for the coast for the week-end.

The address had been given as Mason Road, number 57. And the street map showed it as a small road off the Brighton Road. The sun was still warm and children played in the streets, and when he turned into Mason Road he looked for the numbers. The odd numbers were on the other side, and 57 was the last but one. They were small terraced houses and number 57 was obviously well cared for. The paint was clean and there was a window-box of begonias and trailing ivy. The brass numerals on the door and the lion's-head knocker shone bright and clear. He knocked on the door and stood away as he waited.

An old man answered the door. White haired but a child's complexion. He stood with his head askew because one eye was obviously blind.

"Who's that?"

"My name's Bailey, and I wondered if you could help me."

"What about?"

"I'm trying to trace Mr. and Mrs. Walters who used to live here."

The good blue eye looked him over and the old man held the door-frame to maintain his balance.

"What d'you want 'em for?"

"I wanted to speak to them about their son."

"Which son would that be?"

"James Fuller Walters."

The old man looked down at his camel-hair slippers and then back at Bailey's face.

"You'd better come in, mister, you'd better come in."

And he turned and shuffled into the dimness of the small house, leaving Bailey to close the door behind him. It was a neat little parlour and the black and white TV flickered in the corner without sound. The old man stood behind the tall arm-chair, his hands holding its back for support. He looked at Bailey as he spoke.

"Are you from the social security?"

"No. I just wanted some details."

The old man shook his head slowly.

"There ain't no details. He's dead."

"Why didn't you come forward?"

"I don't know what you mean. We went to the hospital straight away. But it was too late."

"When was this?"

"October. The twenty-first of October, 1944."

The old man's lips trembled and Bailey controlled his impatience to hear the details. "How about I make you a cuppa, Dad?"

"All right, but not too heavy-handed with the sugar."

When he had poured out the tea he sat facing the old man.

"How old was your boy when he died?"

"He were just coming up to twenty-five."

"You're Mr. Walters, his father?"

"I am that. He was a good lad, no trouble to me or his Ma."

"What happened?"

"He were on leave. Two more days to go. He went up to town with that girl. His Ma always said she were a bad influence."

"And what happened?"

"They were hit by the V2 at Marble Arch. The girl was killed outright but they brought 'im back to the Mayday. He only lasted another three days. His legs were gone."

"And you live on your own?"

"Since Ma died, yes. Seven years now. But I manages. I'm independent."

"What did your son look like, Mr. Walters?"

"He were a very good-looking little lad. Tall, dark red hair—auburn they calls it—just like Ma's, and blue eyes and freckles all over his face. He didn't like them. The girls teased him about 'em."

Bailey reached inside his jacket pocket and pulled out his wallet. He handed the photograph of Walters to the old man.

"Have you ever seen that man before, Mr. Walters? Have a good look."

"I'll need me specs then, they're over there on the sideboard if you'll get 'em. And you'd better put the light on while you're up."

Bailey had handed him his glasses and the old man had looked carefully at the photograph, holding it at arm's length and slowly bringing it closer.

"Oh ah. I've seen 'im lots of times. He's on the telly. Used to be always goin' on about the blacks. Funny name 'e 'ad. Old-fashioned. Now what was it." He snapped his thin fingers. "I know. It was Enoch. Ought to ha' been Prime Minister."

He handed the picture back to Bailey who glanced at it as he slid it into his wallet. There *was* a resemblance to Enoch Powell. The watching eyes. The square jaw and the quiff of dark hair.

He had sat chatting with the old man for another half-hour. He had never asked the reason for the visit.

• • •

He phoned Murphy at eleven the next day. He told Bailey to come to Victoria Street at once. Murphy had Lovegrove with him when Bailey was shown into his office. The Foreign Office man had been brought from the Oval Test Match and was suitably annoyed. Murphy swept his protests aside: "It was you who insisted that we keep it open, Lovegrove. And you were right. So let's hear the story." He waved at Bailey.

"Whoever the dead man is, he isn't James Fuller Walters. The real Walters died late in 1944 and is buried in the local churchyard."

"There was a phoney application for a passport in the dead man's name, yes?"

"Yes, sir."

Murphy lifted his eyebrows at the FO man. "You really will have to sort out your passports people."

Lovegrove's face flushed with anger. "We've got every reasonable check you could have. If we went any further we should have complaints about being the Gestapo or about delays in issuing passports." He turned to Bailey. "Somebody will have signed the bloody photograph—a doctor or a JP. Have you checked that?"

Bailey nodded. "Yes, it was Randolph Slessor, MP."

Lovegrove stopped biting a nail. "And that's your side Murphy—another of your bloody crypto-Communists. Why don't you fix the bastards?"

Murphy was too professional and too interested in the new information to play politics with the FO man, and he leaned forward towards Bailey.

"OK. You've made your point. That's a good enough reason. A faked passport application off the details of a dead man. Typical KGB. Now find out who Walters really was, and what he was up to."

• • •

Bailey caught the Paris plane and the MI6 man met him at de Gaulle. They sat in the restaurant as rain lashed the big windows, driven by the wind.

"It's a legitimate gallery. Small. Mainly drawings and water colours. It's owned and run by a woman, Monique

Fleury. Lives in a studio flat over the gallery. Just about makes a living. She's rather nice."

"And why is she co-operating with the KGB?"

"I think their contact man is screwing her."

"And it's just a letter-box?"

"As far as I know. The French don't take it too seriously."

"Who controls the surveillance?"

"The SDCE, but they don't do much. I've been watching it more than they have because the gallery seems to attract a lot of English people. Mainly youngsters."

"Does she know she is under suspicion?"

"I shouldn't think so."

"What's the name of her KGB contact?"

"He's low grade. A KGB lieutenant working as the Third Secretary's secretary. It's a Polish name, Siwecki. Andrei Siwecki."

"Old, young, or what?"

"About thirty-two or thirty-three."

"And the woman?"

"She's thirty-five, but looks younger."

"Where have you booked me in?"

"The George Cinq."

• • •

Bailey had watched the gallery for two days armed with a poor photograph of Siwecki. He had actually seen him twice before he recognized him the third time.

On the third day Bailey had wandered into the gallery. He had rather liked the crayon portraits, and the pale washes of the water-colour landscapes were beautifully evocative of Provence in all the seasons. The young woman who offered him a catalogue had said,

"Did any of them appeal to you, m'sieur?"

"Yes. Every single one. Except that one." And he pointed at a water-colour of stark flat fields and the ominous black clouds that seemed to be bursting with snow. The fields were so muddy and wet that he could feel it through the rubber soles of his shoes.

The girl laughed. "You're making the mistake of not liking the picture because it portrays winter and wetness."

He smiled back at her. "They're all too expensive for me."

Her arms went out and her shoulders up in a Gallic shrug. "But you don't know the prices."

"They would be too dear."

She crooked a finger. "Come with me." She walked over to the far corner, and pointed at a pair of small water-colours. One was of a chestnut leaf. Pale yellow and bright green against the sun, its veins like delicate bones. The other was of a chestnut in its open shell. Rich brownish red, shining as if it were fresh polished, the white pith soapy and soft as it cradled the swollen nut.

"How much each do you think?"

He shrugged. "I genuinely have no idea."

"Do you smoke?"

"Yes."

"How many packets a day?"

"Three."

Her face lit up. "There you are, for two and a half weeks' smoking you could have a lovely picture. Painted with skill and love. And you would be healthier too."

He smiled at her amiably. "Which one shall I have, Mam'selle?"

She stamped her foot: "Do they not touch you? Your mind, your heart, your soul?"

"People do that for me. Not paintings."

She stood quite still, her mouth open to speak, her teeth even and white. The she closed her mouth.

"You are, of course, quite right. I apologize."

She looked at him, her head on one side, childlike. "You've got an accent. English or German?"

"English."

She smiled. "It's very attractive."

He smiled back at her. "In that case I'll ask you to have dinner with me tonight."

"Tonight the gallery has a little "vernissage" for the water-colour artist." She smiled as she saw his disappointment, "But of course you could come and join us. There will be about thirty all told. Nothing very special."

"Maybe I should be in the way."

The fine eyebrows went up. "We start at eight. Try and

come." And she turned away dismissively to straighten a small pile of catalogues on the teak table.

• • •

He had arrived at eight-thirty and there was music playing over the hubbub of conversation and laughter. The girl was laughing in a circle of men and girls who were listening to a man with a dark beard who was drawing in the air with slender delicate hands. Siwecki was in the group, smiling at the gesticulating man, his arm round the girl's slim waist.

The young man who had let him in took him over to the girl. She broke away from the circle and took him to the table of drinks. And with a glass of white wine she led him back to her circle.

"I don't even know your name."

"Nick. Nicholas Bailey. And yours?"

"Monique Fleury."

"Nicholas, meet Anne-Marie, up and coming sculptress. Anton, he carves wood. Jean-Paul, photography—nude girls. Pierre Robin, art critic, and Andrei Siwecki, cultural attaché for Red Russia."

Bailey had bowed and smiled round the circle and the conversation went on. It was all shop. The sagas of worthless pictures sold, and genius unrecognized, of carping critics and greedy dealers.

He had left about ten and the girl had held his hand as she walked him to the door. As he stood there he said, "I'll buy the leaf painting." She clapped her hands. "That's fine. I'll tell Paulette, who painted it. She'll be so pleased."

"How about I call for it about mid-day and I take you to lunch?"

She nodded. "That's fine. I'll look forward to that."

• • •

He had brought her back to the restaurant at the George Clinq and he had quizzed her, as they ate, about the problems of running a small gallery.

Finally she asked him: "And what do you do, Nick?"

"Guess."

She half-closed the blue eyes: "Something to do with power. A politician or a lawyer."

He shook his head, smiling.

"So. A soldier or maybe a policeman."

He laughed. "I'm an insurance assessor."

"What on earth is that?"

"If people claim on a loss I check to see that what we pay is a fair amount."

She smiled, and said, "Exactly. Policeman, judge and jury all rolled into one, deciding the fate of innocent citizens."

"They aren't always innocent."

"Are any of us innocent any more, Nicholas?"

"Can you come out for dinner tonight?"

She slowly shook her head. "Andrei is taking me to dinner."

"Is he your lover?"

She closed one eye and looked at him speculatively. "I suppose that is how my friends would describe him, and maybe my mother, because it sounds romantic."

"Isn't it romantic?"

She slowly shook her head. "No. Not really, we just go to bed together. It's maybe more than that but that is the basis."

"And no love, on either side?"

She moved glasses around on the table as she considered her reply. She looked up at him. "Andrei is married. His wife is in Moscow; she is the hostage so that he doesn't defect. He is charming, intelligent and good company. And he makes love to me like a wild animal."

She smiled as she saw his face. "And now I've spoilt it all. The fairy princess changes into a frog."

He put his hand across the table and instantly her hand turned up to his, her fingers spread to lace through his.

"What sort of man is he?"

She put her head on one side as she looked at him quizzically.

"Quite civilized, intelligent, human, hypocritical, ambitious, a liar." She smiled. "Just a normal, slightly selfish man."

Bailey noted that the girl had not mentioned Siwecki's good looks.

"It's a Polish name, isn't it?"

"I think his father was Polish and fought with the Russians in World War II. He's Russian himself."

"What does he do?"

"God knows, he's a secretary to some embassy official. You never know with Soviet officials what they're up to."

His hand slid up to hold her slim waist. "I'm leaving Paris tomorrow, can I call you when I come back?"

She smiled at him warmly: "Of course you can. I shall look forward to that."

• • •

It was early evening when the train pulled into Périgueux and Bailey had enquired the way to the Hotel Domino. He had walked with his light case down to the Place Francheville and had claimed his booking for three nights.

After eating he had checked the address of the local paper and had walked around the town. The streets were busy and the people looked prosperous. In the late evening sun, people sat under the café awnings as if it were a daily routine. There were chess players, men playing draughts and couples with café-filtres dripping slowly into clouded glasses. And from time to time there was the monotonous thudding of a disco. He walked down to the bank of the river where couples sat, and men were fishing, solitary on their little canvas stools with bait-cans and keep-nets at their feet. There were many obvious tourists in the town and he had a feeling of not belonging because his visit was not for pleasure. He read a few pages of a paperback copy of Montaigne's essays in bed, and was asleep well before midnight.

• • •

Next morning at the offices of *Le Courier Français–Périgord* he asked to see the editor, and three minutes later he was shown into the small office. The editor was a young man in his middle thirties and he waved Bailey to a leather chair in front of the old-fashioned desk.

"Prévert, monsieur, Jacques Prévert, editor-in-chief. How can I help you, M'sieur Bailey?"

Bailey pulled out the brown envelope and slid out the cutting and passed it across the desk to Prévert.

"Could you tell me if that is from your journal, Monsieur Prévert?"

The young man smiled as he looked at the picture.

"Yes, but we've improved our quality of newsprint since then. It's very old."

He looked across at Bailey, his eyebrows raised quizzically. "What else do you want to know?"

"I wonder if you could help me identify any of the people in the photograph."

Prévert looked down at the cutting. "A few. But Michaux could. I expect he took the photograph."

And he pressed one of the buttons on his desk and leaned back.

"Is it important?"

"Not really. But it's important to me."

And then the door opened and an elderly man with a mass of yellow-white hair came in, his spectacles pushed up to his forehead. Prévert pointed at the cutting.

"Is this one of yours, André?"

The old man picked up the paper and pulled down his spectacles and examined the picture.

"Yes, chief. It must have been '52 or '53."

"Do you recognize any of the people?"

The old man nodded. "Some of them."

He pointed at one of the fuzzy, indistinct faces. "That's Devereux, Michel, the brother of Jean-Luc and . . ." He stood upright, one hand massaging his hip. ". . . This was a commemorative service, here at Périgueux. . . ." He turned to Bailey. ". . . we've stopped having them now, but we used to have them every year until about '70 or '71. . . ." He pointed at the picture. ". . . They had the Resistance people in the first few rows and then the old soldiers . . . very impressive it was too." He paused, caught up in his thoughts, and Bailey looked across at Prévert.

"Maybe I could take M'sieur Michaux for a coffee and have a chat about the people who are in the photograph."

Prévert nodded, smiling. "An excellent idea."

"Thanks for your help."

"You're welcome. By the way, what's your interest?"

"Oh, it's just for the friend of a friend."

Prévert half-smiled in tolerant disbelief as he stood up to shake hands.

• • •

The old man leaned with his arms on the table, looking at the photograph, and Bailey opened the writing-pad and waited.

"Going from left to right—the front row. First there's old Frenez. He's a lawyer from Angoulême. Pots of money and a great big house. Then there's Servagnat—he's dead now. Next to him there's Devereux, he's there representing his brother Jean-Luc who was arrested by the Germans, executed in Dachau in '45.

"Then we've got the widow Chaland and her daughter, now what's her name—can't remember. Then there's Mangeul the chemist, he was one of Devereux's men. I can't identify the next one. And then we've got that bastard Bonnier—he came down from Paris. Never misses the ceremony. He's in the top brass of the Communists in Paris. I don't know what he does.

"At the back we've got the local worthies, the mayor and the rest of them. And this little bunch are the ex-soldiers of both wars. I can't make out any of their faces."

"Have you got the negative still, m'sieur?"

"No. When we moved to the new building we had a big clear out. There's very little left before 1965."

"Did the Resistance do much in this area?"

"Jesus, they did. They really harassed the Germans. But the Boche got their own back in the end. Most of the Resistance people were caught eventually and shipped off to Germany. Most of them were executed. Some just never came back. Those who survived never really settled down. Frenez and Bonnier are the exceptions. There were a few suicides, a murder, and at least two of them are in the asylum at Bordeaux. Something happened to those people when it was all over. And there were years of bitter argument about whether the Resistance didn't make things worse for the civilian population."

"Who was the local leader of the Resistance?"

"Oh, that was Chaland. No doubt about that. A young fellow, not local. I'd say from his accent that he was from Lyons. He'd had training in England for the work. There were rumours that he was English but I don't think so. I used to see him in Périgueux from time to time."

"What's he doing now?"

"He's dead, my friend. The woman in the picture with the little girl. That is his widow and the child is their daughter. He was killed by the Germans. They picked him up during a Resistance raid on a Gestapo HQ over the other side of the river. He was shipped off to Natzweiler and he was executed there like the rest of them. He's the real local hero. His widow has a state pension. She was something to do with the Resistance or the Maquis. She's much respected in these parts. Doesn't mix much, never married again, although she had plenty of offers."

"Where does she live?"

"In Brantôme, not far from the bridge. I don't know the actual address but any of the locals can tell you."

"Were there any Englishmen in these groups?"

"Oh, yes. Three or four. They were mainly with Bonnier's maquis. Teaching them tactics and how to use explosives and weapons. Bonnier could tell you all about them."

• • •

The white walls were high, and swept down, white-painted, to the tall iron-work gate where wrought-iron ivy leaves supported a cross of Lorraine. There was a paved area instead of a garden, with tubs of geraniums and lobelia. The blue house door was standing ajar, and Bailey pushed the brass bell button and waited.

The girl who came to the door was breathtakingly beautiful. Long black hair and hazel eyes, a neat nose and a full mouth that revealed white, even teeth.

"I wonder if I could speak to Madame Chaland?"

The girl looked at him for a few moments before she spoke. "Maman is not here. She's at the cottage."

"Would it be possible to visit her there?"

"Why do you want to speak to her?"

"I wanted her help."

"Is your accent English?"

"Yes."

"You are English?"

"Yes."

The girl hesitated. "Is it about Maman's pension?"

"No. It's nothing to do with that."

"She'll be back tomorrow. Can it wait until then?"

"It could, but I'm only here for two days, and there are other people I would like to talk to after I've talked to your mother."

She looked at him searchingly for a moment and then stood aside. "You'd better come in for a moment and I will speak to Maman on the telephone."

The room was dark, but soothing rather than gloomy. The highly polished parquet floor had a patina that rivalled the polish of the small Blüthner grand piano. The furniture was bourgeois French, solid and well made. The girl had waved him to a chair and walked through to the next room. He could hear her voice on the telephone but it wasn't loud enough for him to hear what she was saying.

He was looking at the music that lay open on the piano as she came back into the room. The title was "Intermezzo in E Flat" and the composer was Brahms. The girl stood there looking at him, her eyes alight.

"You play the piano?"

He shook his head, and the light faded from her eyes.

"Would you play for me?"

She hesitated briefly, then, "Of course, but a few bars only because Maman says to go over with you now."

She sat at the piano, suddenly oblivious of everything else. The long elegant fingers were poised for a moment and then softly the melting notes took over, and for the first time in his life Bailey wished he knew something about music. And despite the honey music he was only aware of the lovely tanned arms and the black hair, and the brown curved cheek and the half-open lips. The long black eye-lashes closed for a moment as she lifted her hands from the keyboard. He said how beautiful it was as she slid back the piano stool and stood up, and she smiled a smile from right inside her that showed that she knew that there had been no touching of minds or feelings.

She lifted a linen handbag from an armchair and slid a key ring on to her finger and looked at him.

"Shall we go?"

"It's very kind of you."

• • •

The small Fiat had needed petrol, and as they waited at the pump he said: "How far is the cottage?"

"Oh, not far, it's at Puy Henry. We shall be there in a quarter of an hour."

As she turned out on to the main road she said, "You may find my mother a little strange perhaps. She may seem aloof. When my father was killed it was really the end of her life. She made another life for my sake but it's not the same."

"Are you going to be a musician? Professionally, I mean?"

She laughed. "I *am* a professional musician."

"I'm sorry. I know nothing about music."

"Not any kind of music?"

"Well, jazz or dance tunes."

"Jazz is music. We turn left here, and you'd better hold on to something, it's a bumpy ride up to the farm. But the track only used to go part way and the new bit saves us walking."

She brought the small car to a sweeping stop that threw up a cloud of dust. They were outside a typical Dordogne farm cottage and the door stood open.

The woman inside was shorter than her daughter and there were cards laid out on the rough table. She was playing patience.

She looked up as they came in and she stood up, her face solemn and composed.

"Chantal said you had not introduced yourself." And she made it sound like a discourtesy.

"I'm sorry. My name is Bailey. Nicholas Bailey. It is very good of you to see me."

She stood still, her hands clasped in front of her, her eyes guarded. "What is it you wanted to talk about?"

"They told me at the *Courier Français* that your late husband was the head of the Resistance in this area. I wondered if you remembered any of the Englishmen who were here with the Resistance."

"It's a long time ago, m'sieur."

"I know. It was just a hope. Just a chance."

The woman looked at her daughter. "There is some wine in the kitchen. Bring us some glasses, darling."

She waved Bailey to one of the uncomfortable chairs, and sat opposite to him.

"There were two or three Englishmen. Have you got any idea of the name you are interested in?"

"It could be Walters. James Walters."

She rested her chin on her hand. "I don't recall that name. There were two or three officers dropped in this area. They were military instructors and I don't remember their names. Maybe SOE could help you."

"I see. Maybe they could help."

There was a silence that was broken by the girl returning with the wine and the glasses. He looked across at the woman.

"They told me at the newspaper that you worked in the Resistance."

"I worked with my husband. I was not important."

Bailey felt a tension in the silence as they sipped the wine. He felt a compelling burden to break the silence and he was more used to applying such pressure to others.

"I understand your husband was a great hero in these parts?"

"He still is. He was a brave man."

There was no point in continuing and Bailey pushed back his chair. "It was good of you to see me, madame."

She stood up as if to ensure that he would go.

"Not at all, m'sieur. I hope you find the help you want from others."

She held out her hand, and it was warm and dry to the touch. She didn't come out to see them off but she had kissed her daughter affectionately.

The girl had driven him back to his hotel and had politely declined his invitation to dinner.

• • •

Frenez had been off-hand on the 'phone but he agreed to see him immediately after lunch. Bailey had walked from the railway station to check where Frenez's offices were, and then had had soup and a coffee at a bistro.

The small waiting-room at Frenez's offices was well appointed. None of the gloom of most country lawyers' offices. There were water-colour landscapes on the walls and a photograph of de Gaulle. He had waited for half an hour before the middle-aged secretary had shown him into the inner office.

Frenez had white hair, but it only enhanced his good looks. He was on the telephone and he waved with his long cigarette holder for Bailey to sit in the chair opposite.

". . . If that is what the *juge d'instruction* requires that is what you will do. . . . No, my friend, I shall not. I use my influence in court and nowhere else . . . there is no question of that. I shall see you in court." And the receiver crashed back in its rest.

"What's the trouble, m'sieur?"

"There's no trouble. You said you would see me. My name's Bailey."

"Of course. Of course. What can I do for you?"

Frenez had a resigned air that Bailey felt he must use when listening to importunate litigants.

"I wanted to ask if you could remember the names of the Englishmen who worked in the Resistance in this area."

"Alive or dead?"

"Alive."

"With the Resistance or the maquis?"

"Weren't they the same?"

Frenez screwed up his eyes as he looked at Bailey.

"Far from it."

"But they both had Englishmen serving with them?"

"The maquis certainly did. Two lieutenants and a captain. But you'd have to talk to Bonnier about them."

"You don't remember their names?"

Frenez shook his head. "I may have heard their names but they were of no interest to me. I was in Chaland's command."

"And there were no Englishmen in Chaland's group?"

Frenez shrugged. "If there were you wouldn't know. SOE wouldn't send them if they couldn't pass as Frenchmen. The Germans would have picked them up in a week. We didn't discuss backgrounds, Mr. Bailey. It was better not to know. And Chaland himself was more French than the French themselves."

Bailey took a slow, deep breath before he spoke to take the tension from his voice.

"You mean Chaland wasn't French?"

Frenez leaned back in his chair, looking at Bailey through the cloud of cigarette smoke. It was several seconds before he replied.

"Who are you, Mr. Bailey? What's this interrogation all about?"

"Hardly an interrogation, M'sieur Frenez. More a chat."

Frenez drew on his cigarette and studied Bailey through the haze.

"What are you anyway? Why all the questions?"

"I'm trying to trace what happened to an Englishman who might have been in the Resistance in this area."

"So why not do your checking in London. That's where the records will be."

"When I came out here I wasn't sure that he was anything to do with the Resistance. And I'm still not sure."

"What was his name?"

"I don't know."

Frenez laid down his cigarette in the crystal ash-tray. And as he leaned forward, opening his mouth to speak, Bailey interrupted. "You implied that Chaland might have been English."

The lawyer leaned back again in his chair, tapping a long silver letter-opener on his desk as he looked at Bailey.

"Chaland was English all right. I don't think there is any secret about that."

"Everybody else seems to think he was a Frenchman."

Frenez shrugged. "They wouldn't know, for God's sake. In SOE people had all sorts of names and cover stories. I doubt if Chaland was his real name, but he spoke French like a Frenchman."

"What sort of man was he?"

Frenez held out his hands: "Brave, dedicated, tough, ruthless—a leader."

"And a hero?"

"No doubt about that."

"What happened to him?"

"He led a raid on a Gestapo HQ and they were waiting for him. They shipped him off to Germany. He was executed in a concentration camp."

"Which one?"

"Natzweiler, I think."

"What date was this?"

"He was captured the day de Gaulle marched into Paris, whatever date that was."

"What did he look like?"

"Stocky, average height, brown hair, an ordinary sort of face. He was in his early twenties."

"You knew him well?"

"Yes, my reseau came under his control."

"You got on well?"

For the first time Frenez smiled. "He was a big Boy Scout, but everybody in SOE was like that—apart from that aspect we got on well enough."

"Did he have any enemies?"

The lawyer sighed quietly. "Everybody had enemies in those days. Germans. Frenchmen. He visited me on one occasion and was picked up by the Germans on the way back. He escaped but it was obvious that someone had tipped off the Germans that he was in Limoges."

"Any idea who the traitor was?"

Frenez's shrewd eyes looked at him and the lawyer threw the letter-opener on to the desk as he leaned forward.

"I'd deny it if you repeated it, but I'd say it was Bonnier."

"He was in command of the maquis?"

"Yes. Another brave one, but a Commie, and always

grinding their political axe. Waiting for the big take-over when the Germans left."

"*Did* he take over?"

Frenez stood up, a broad smile on his face. "No, there were others who also made plans for the future. Now I must get on with my work, M'sieur Bailey.

• • •

Bailey had taken the train back to Péregueux and booked a flight from Bordeaux to London the next day.

Chapter Eleven

The Ministry of Defence was never at its most co-operative with Special Branch, and when the subject under discussion was the war-time records of Special Operations Executive the temperature tended to be even lower. Bailey disliked the fruity voice on the other end of the line and he resented the attempt to side-track him.

"Does that mean that all the SOE records were destroyed, Brigadier?"

"Oh no, I said *most* of them were destroyed."

"So some still exist?"

"I imagine so."

"Can you tell me where they are?"

"Can't help you, old boy."

"Would the DMI be able to help, do you think?"

"SOE were in care of the Ministry of Economic Warfare, old chap. Nothing to do with the Army."

"I'll try the DMI all the same."

There was a long pause at the other end as the Army PR man tried to decide how the chips would fall.

"Maybe you should try the Intelligence Corps depot at Ashford."

"Ashford Middlesex or Ashford Kent?"
"Ashford Kent."
"Who would be the man concerned?"
"The *officer* concerned would be Major Wilkins."
"Can you give me his telephone number?"
"What on earth for?"
"So that I can phone him."
"But you don't know him, surely you'll write first."
Bailey hung up secure in the knowledge that the day of the grammar school boy had not yet arrived, no matter what they said.

• • •

The remaining records of SOE occupied ten metal filing cabinets in a Nissen hut at the Intelligence Corps depot and Bailey had been left with a chair and a couple of army issue trestle tables.

All that remained of the records of the SOE operation in the Périgord were twenty files bound together with pink tape.

He had read half-way through the file marked "Parker" before he realized that that was Chaland. He checked back on the first operational order and the cover name was Levoisier.

There was a duplicated Official Secrets Act form with a faded signature—"C du P Parker."

A bundle of Part II Orders from 2nd Echelon recorded promotions from Lieutenant to Captain and then Major. And there were records of pay passed to an account at Coutts Bank.

There were brown edged signal forms with over a hundred signals from the OC of operation LANTERN.

There was a recommendation for a DSO and the confirmation from the War Office dated September 1944. A letter from the French Ministry of Defence notifying the award of a Croix de Guerre and a copy of a letter from the War Office pointing out that serving British officers were not permitted to accept foreign decorations while hostilities were still being waged.

There were two hand-written letters in already opened white envelopes addressed to Mrs. Parker at an address in Birmingham. Both letters said that the writer was well and in no danger. They were signed "Charlie" and on both envelopes was scrawled in pencil: "Addressee—next of kin—extinct—do not despatch." They were the routine letters written by agents before being dropped in enemy territory so that SOE could send them from time to time to keep next-of-kin quiet and incurious.

There was a short list of personal effects of Mrs. Parker deceased, held in store at Baker Street pending the return of her son and a red crayon note that said "Destroyed Nov. 1946."

Held together with a paperclip were two pieces of paper. The top one was a decoded signal from LANTERN reporting that Chaland had been arrested by the Gestapo in Périgueux and mentioning the possibility that he was either dead or in a German camp. There was an inked note in a neat round hand that pointed out to someone named Fredericks that the security checks had been omitted from the coded signal and that it was therefore suspect.

The second paper was badly typed and said simply: "Charles du Puy Parker not traced during V.A.'s investigation. Can be assumed dead. No next-of-kin. Accrued pay of £207.14.3 passed to GSO II GHQ Home Forces, Hounslow."

• • •

Bailey parked the hired car just past the gate to the garden. It had taken him an hour from Hanover and twenty minutes to find the cottage just outside Hildesheim on the road to Peine. The cottage was small and cosy looking, like an illustration from a children's book. The tall privet hedge was broken by a small white gate, and Bailey walked through following the path to the front door. A sleek and friendly dachshund came round the corner of the cottage from the garden at the rear, and when there was no answer to his knock he walked slowly round to the back of the house.

A man was lying on a canvas shaded settee, his hand reaching for a glass beside him on the lawn. At Bailey's cough he turned his head and the long legs swung to the ground.

"Herr Krugman?"

"What do you want?"

"They told me at Hanover that you might be able to help me."

"Who told you that?"

"The Oberbürgermeister."

Krugman stood up slowly, stretching his arms lazily.

"What is it you want?"

"I wanted some information about an Englishman who was in Natzweiler while you were Commandant."

The tanned face exaggerated the blue eyes, and the deep lines beside the leathery lips were set in anger. The big fist shook slowly, emphasizing the words. "I've made all the statements to journalists that I'm going to make so get the hell out of here."

The big man came menacingly forward but Bailey stood his ground. When the man was two feet away he said, "I'm not a journalist. I'm a British official and I require some information about a British officer who may have been murdered in Natzweiler concentration camp."

Bubbles of saliva on his lips marked the man's anger. His voice trembled with rage: "Read the record of my trial. It's all there. You bastards jailed me for fifteen years. Now it's over and Germans don't lick British arses any longer."

"I've read the trial testimony, Herr Krugman. Three British girls of SOE were executed in your camp. I am enquiring about a British officer of SOE who may also have been executed."

"The Gestapo did the executions, not me. I administered the prison camp. I didn't choose the prisoners or sentence them."

"Herr Krugman, I had better explain. You may not be able to help me, but if I suspect you are not co-operating with me I shall apply to the War Crimes Commission for their assistance. I don't mind which way we do it."

Krugman stood, hands on hips, head aggressively thrust forward, his massive chest heaving within the dark blue jersey, his eyes like a leopard's, on Bailey's face. Then suddenly he relaxed, and pointing to a white chair he sat back on the swinging garden seat and reached for his drink.

"What was the man's name?"

"Chaland. Charles Chaland."

Krugman's arm stopped with the glass half-way to his mouth. "But he wasn't English. He was French. And he wasn't executed."

"You remember him?"

"Indeed I do."

"Tell me about him."

Krugman wiped his mouth with the back of his hand and stood up.

"Come inside. We'll go in my study."

A young man was eating ice-cream in the kitchen and he stood up awkwardly as the two men walked through. Krugman half-turned in the hall: "My son Siegfried. He was the only one who stuck by me."

Krugman pushed open a door and pointed to a leather armchair and opened a metal filing cabinet. After a few minutes searching he brought out a tattered old-fashioned ledger with a leather half-binding. He sat down at the desk and slowly turned the pages, his fingers tracing down lists of names.

"Yes, here it is. He was brought to the camp on 9 September 1944. Handed over by SS Obergruppenführer Kaldor. Arrested as an Allied agent in Périgueux, France, responsible for murder of unnamed German officers. Solitary confinement. To await disposal instructions from Berlin. He was released from solitary 7 October 1944, on instructions of RSHA Berlin. On 3 November hospitalized. No further entries."

Krugman looked up at Bailey. "Is he the man you wanted to check on?"

"I think so. What was he treated for in hospital?"

Krugman closed the ledger and leaned back. "He'd been in Gestapo hands and he was in bad shape. I visited prisoners in solitary every other day. He was not allowed to talk and only minimal rations. He had a lot of fractures. Arms, hands, fingers and feet were smashed up."

"What happened after he came out of hospital?"

"He didn't come out."

"You mean he died?"

"No. Do you know anything about how the camps were run?"

"Only what's common knowledge."

Krugman looked towards the window where the sun shone through the pale green leaves of virginia creeper that clung to the glass. Then he looked back at Bailey.

"I got a load of shrapnel in my belly outside Stalingrad and when I was fit I was posted to Natzweiler as Commandant. I hated it but I was glad to have a soft job. After a few months I was indifferent to what went on. You won't believe it but the really brutal people were the 'Kapos'—the prisoners who were in charge of other prisoners. And in most camps, Dachau, Belsen, the 'Kapos' were all Commies. It was the same at Natzweiler. The Reds ran the camp. They administered rations, discipline in the huts and medical supplies. They shared out the women prisoners. We let them get on with it. It was the Commies who took over Chaland. They fixed for the hospital treatment for him and he dropped out of sight. But I can tell you he was not executed. Not by me or my staff or by the Gestapo men."

There was a long silence as both men looked at each other. It was Bailey who broke the silence.

"What happened to you?"

"I was arrested by the Americans. I was in a camp for a year and then I was tried and found guilty. I served fifteen years and then I was released. I get an army disability pension and now I sell insurance. My wife divorced me when I was in jail. The boy came to see me in jail and has lived with me since I got out. He's a good boy."

"What do you think happened to Chaland?"

Krugman shook his head. "The camp was in chaos long before the Americans got there. I would have thought Chaland would have been repatriated by the French."

"Were there many French Resistance people in Natzweiler?"

"Yes, several. And British."

"What happened to the British?"

"They were executed on Gestapo orders."

"And the girls?"

"They were executed too."

"How?"

"The Gestapo doctor injected phenol and they were cremated."

"Still alive?"

"That's what the prosecution said."

"And were the French agents executed?"

"Most of them."

"Can you give me the names of the French who were not executed?"

Krugman opened the ledger and turned the pages.

"Executed were—La Roche, Devereux, Martinu, Cordez and Passy. Not executed—Scavron, Toulet, Bonnier and Gautier."

"Do you remember Bonnier?"

"Vaguely. He was one of the 'Kapos.'"

• • •

It was the beginning of autumn, and brown leaves swirled along the pavements in front of the shops in the Champs-Elysées, and although it was only six-thirty the daylight was already going, and the lights were on in shop windows and cafés. Then he saw her, picking her way through the tables towards him. She sat down breathlessly, smiling as she loosened her scarf and pushed back her hair over her shoulders.

"So the wandering boy is back. I thought we had lost you forever."

"It took me longer than I expected. I'm glad you could come."

She smiled: "An hour. That's all."

"What'll you have?"

"Just a coffee."

When the drinks had arrived Bailey said: "How are things with you and the gallery?"

"I'm fine; the gallery just keeps its head above water."

"And how's lover boy?"

She smiled: "Andrei? He's OK."

"Would you do me a favour?"

One hazel eye closed as her head tilted on one side to look at his face.

"A lot of troubles start with a question like that."

"No trouble. I promise."

"OK What's the favour?"

"Have you ever heard of a man named Bonnier?"

"Michel Bonnier?"

"Yes."

"So who hasn't heard of him. He's deputy something or other of the Communist Party."

"Could you get me an introduction to him?"

The smile faded slowly and the colour went from her cheeks. "Why me?" she whispered.

"I thought you could. Through Siwecki perhaps."

"Why don't you contact Bonnier yourself?"

"Because I don't know him. And I need his help but I don't think he would co-operate with *me*."

"What are you, Nicholas?" she said softly. "You're not an insurance man are you?"

"In a kind of a way I am. It was a half-truth."

"The other half of a half-truth must be a half-lie."

"I'm afraid so."

"And you expect me to tell half-lies for you?"

"No. I'll tell you the substance of what I'm trying to find out. Providing you don't tell Siwecki."

"Why should I compromise my relationship with him for your sake?"

"Because he compromises his relationship with you."

"How?"

"You get letters and packages left at your gallery which you give to Siwecki. Yes?"

"Yes. Just paperbacks—*livres de poche*."

"They'll have coded messages in them, Monique. That's a standard KGB device. They'll probably be pin codes."

"What the hell are they?"

"You just put pin-pricks in letters or words. It's crude and simple."

"I don't believe it."

"You do, my love. You'd rather not believe it, but you do.

Your gallery is a dead-letter box for the KGB in Paris. And Siwecki is a junior officer in the KGB."

"How do you know all this?"

"The French Security people know about it and told their opposite numbers in London."

"Is this the 'Deuxième Bureau'?"

"No, an outfit called SDECE."

"Christ, I've heard of them, they're tough aren't they?"

He nodded. "I could put that straight for you."

"And what about Siwecki?"

"Except for the introduction to Bonnier, nothing need affect him."

"But what about when the paperbacks come in future?"

"You take them but you don't tell Siwecki for twenty-four hours. Then you just hand 'em over to him as you usually do."

"Why the delay?"

"So that SDECE can have a look at them first."

"But they'll be in my office at the gallery."

"That's OK."

"You mean . . ."

"I mean you just go on as before. Just the delay of a day. Nothing more."

She looked absent-mindedly round the restaurant and then sighed as she looked back at him.

"It's a horrible world, isn't it?"

His hand covered hers and there were tears brimming at her eyes.

"Not really. Not if we don't ask too much of our friends."

"But Andrei must have known it could make trouble for me."

"He's not very experienced, I expect, and he doesn't think for a moment that he's been spotted. The Russians live in a world of their own. Anyway I'll make clear to SDECE that you had no idea what's been going on. They wouldn't want you to stop, it would make the Russians suspicious."

"And how do I treat Andrei?"

"The same as ever. If you like him, OK. If not, downgrade him, or give him the chop altogether."

"But he will sense the difference."

Bailey slowly shook his head. "No he won't. He's not that perceptive."

She sipped from the already empty cup and Bailey waved to a waitress and was silent until she had brought more coffee.

"Will you help me with Bonnier?"

She looked up at his face. "When I was coming here tonight I was happy. I was looking forward to seeing you again. And afterwards there was Andrei. And now there's *nothing* to be happy about. Two people I liked aren't what they seemed."

His index finger stroked the back of her hand. "Nobody's what they seem, my love. Not even you."

She looked up quickly. "In what way am I not what I seem?"

"When your friends, or Siwecki or me, think of you we make an image that is partly our own thinking. We give you characteristics that you don't have because it would be nice, or tidy, or convenient to us, to have it so. We cast you for *our* mental film not your own. So we distort you. Maybe with love, maybe with indifference. So you are not what you seem because we make it so."

And as he said the words out loud he knew that he had been thinking for hours of the girl in the orange dress in Brantôme. A girl whose interest in him vanished the moment she realized that he knew nothing of music. And despite knowing that, and all the other signs of indifference on her part, he longed to be with her. His heart felt literally heavy. Except that she was beautiful and graceful and talented he knew nothing about her but he was drawn to her as surely as steel is drawn to a magnet. Monique Fleury brought him back to earth.

"What shall I say to Andrei about why you want to see Bonnier?"

"Tell him I want to trace a relative, a man who might have been in the Resistance in the same area as Bonnier."

"Just that?"

"Yes."

She was screwing up the paper from the sugar cubes and watching as the twisted ball of paper slowly expanded in the palm of her hand. Without looking up she said, "Are you married?"

"No."

"Divorced?"

"Yes."

"In love?"

He hesitated just too long and she looked at him smiling. "Now it's my turn to tell fortunes. You *do* love someone, but she doesn't love you."

When she looked at his face she saw that her barb had gone deep and she leaned forward. "I'm sorry. That was unkind. What's her name?"

"Chantal."

"Is she French?"

"Yes."

"Where did you meet her?"

"A few days ago in Périgueux."

"What's so special about her?"

"I don't know. It just happened. I only saw her for a couple of hours, and I can't forget her."

"Was she interested?"

"Not the slightest."

She looked at her watch. "I'll have to go, Nick. I'll phone you later tonight or early tomorrow."

• • •

The meeting had been arranged for four o'clock and Bailey stood in the reception area looking at the photographs of Soviet dignitaries pressing buttons to start things, waving to groups of workers, greeting returned spacemen, and examining Olympic medals on athletes. Then a large man stood half out of one of the office doors and waved him inside.

It would have been impossible to visualize Bonnier as a Resistance fighter were it not for the photograph on the wall where he was standing in a line of men facing de Gaulle, ready to receive one of the medals held on a cushion by an aide. Now his face was red, unhealthily red, the colour that overweight men get from high blood pressure. He wore a superb blue suit that had been designed to minimize the fat belly and emphasize the broad shoulders. He breathed heavily as he sat with one big paw cradled in the other, making himself comfortable in the creaking chair.

"Well, my friend, you wanted to speak to me." And the piggy eyes held all the left-over residue from a hundred negotiations with powerful opponents.

"I wanted to ask you about a man who I think was in the Resistance with you."

The big cigar described an arc and the red face creased into a smile and his laugh became a wheezing cough. "The whole world was in the Resistance, comrade. After the Germans had gone. Who was your claimant?"

"Chaland. Charles Chaland."

The shrewd eyes looked quickly away towards the windows, and then he looked back at Bailey.

"What about him?"

"Was he in the Resistance?"

Bonnier nodded. "Yes, he was."

"Could you tell me something about him?"

Bonnier leaned back and swiveled his chair so that he was sideways on to the desk.

"He was a very brave man. There's no doubt about that."

"Did you like him?"

Bonnier pursed his lips. "They weren't days for liking, comrade. They were days for fighting the Germans. He was a good leader. We co-operated."

"Was he a Communist?"

Bonnier swung round to look at Bailey. "You can't be serious. He had no interest in politics at all, that's why he was so successful with such a big group. He was only interested in fighting the Boche."

"And his wife?"

"What about her?"

"Was he fond of her?"

Bonnier tapped the long ash off his cigar. "Yes, he was fond of her all right."

"What happened to him?"

"He was caught by the Gestapo and they almost killed him. They sent him to a camp."

"What did they do to him?"

"The Gestapo you mean?"

"Yes."

"I only saw him for a few minutes that night and he was unconscious then. His arms were broken and there were bones sticking out of his feet. He had a bad time. They were in a hurry, the bastards."

"How did you come to be there?"

"I'd been arrested too but they didn't bother with the likes of me when they'd got him. I got the cold bath treatment but they were all working on Chaland. I saw him two nights later when we were put on the railway wagons for Germany. After we got there I didn't see him for about two months. He was a sick man but we got him some medical treatment."

"Was he executed?"

Bonnier carefully moved a pile of papers to make room for his arm on the desk. "No, he wasn't executed."

"What happened to him?"

"I don't know, the camp was in turmoil in the last few weeks. It was every man for himself."

"You went by rail to Germany?"

"Yes."

"In the same truck as Chaland?"

"Yes. I looked after him on the journey. So did Devereux. They shot Devereux a month after we got there."

"You were a 'Kapo' at Natzweiler?"

"What makes you think that, comrade?"

"I thought the Communists ran the camps on a day-to-day basis."

"Who gave you that bullshit?"

"I've seen reports on those lines. And Krugman said so too."

"Just the Germans looking for someone to share the blame, my friend. The Communists are everybody's bogymen."

"Krugman said that you had helped to ensure that Chaland got medical treatment."

"Sure I did. We were comrades." He held up his massive hand, smiling. "And that *doesn't* mean he was a Communist."

"Do you know M'sieur Frenez?"

"I knew him, but not well. He was part of Chaland's SOE units."

"He told me that somebody tipped off the Germans on one occasion when Chaland was in Limoges. Have you any idea who that could have been?"

"Could have been anybody. The Germans paid informants well. Could have been somebody under pressure from the Germans. They would use members of a man's family as pressure points."

"But you've no idea of who it could be?"

Bonnier slowly stood up, wheezing as he did so. "God knows. Have a look at Frenez himself. I haven't been much help I'm afraid."

"If I needed to talk again would you be willing?"

Bonnier spread his arms, shrugging. "Of course. Just telephone direct."

• • •

The view from the train was of autumn. In a few days summer had suddenly ended and the earth's chemistry had turned the leaves from their dusty summer greens to the colours of sunset and hot metal. Bailey wondered whether his journey to Périgueux was really necessary or if it was just an excuse to see the girl again. He had telephoned Madame Chaland and she had reluctantly agreed to see him.

When he finally stood outside the blue painted door his heart was beating as if he were in danger. It was Madame Chaland herself who opened the door and her mien was not unfriendly. She had walked him through the sitting-room to a small study at the side of the house. Chantal was there and it was a shock when he saw that she was not wearing the orange dress. He had never imagined her in anything else. She was wearing a black wool dress that clung to her body and matched her hair and eyes. She stood up from the table which was half-covered with open music scores and gave him a friendly smile.

"So you're back to Périgueux."

"I'm afraid so. I wanted a chat with your mother." He hesitated, and then said, "How's the music going?"

The fleeting frown underlined the banality of what he had said. And even as he asked the foolish question he had been aware that he had only referred to the music to ingratiate himself. And the form of the question itself had merely underlined his being outside the magic circle. But she saw the embarrassment on his face and smiled. "Oh, lots practice, nothing exciting."

And she picked up one of the scores and made for the door where she stopped for a moment.

"Give me a call, Maman, if you want coffee." And then she was gone.

When he turned to look at her mother, she was looking at him. The same dark eyes were faintly amused. She waved him to one of the chairs.

"I've spoken with Monsieur Frenez and Monsieur Bonnier, and I wondered if you could help me on something?"

"I'll try."

"Frenez told me that somebody had tipped off the Germans that your husband was in Limoges and the Germans had caught him but he had escaped. He suggested in confidence that it might have been Bonnier who was the traitor."

She looked at him in silence for long moments and then said, "And you want to know what I think?"

"Yes."

"Mister Bailey, everybody talks about 'The Resistance.' But it wasn't as clear cut as all that. Even your Special Operations Executive added to the confusion. My husband worked for 'F' section which was different from 'RF' section, another part of SOE which co-operated closely with de Gaulle's Free French. Then there was the maquis—thousands of men who were controlled by nobody but their own leaders. There was a big Communist influence there. Towards the end de Gaulle had sent his own men, French officers, who ignored any British officers or British organizations. And after D-day the people in various parts of the Resistance were not only fighting the Germans but struggling to find a political platform for when France was liberated. So far as I know Bonnier's maquis were the only maquis who co-operated at all with an SOE commander except for arms drops."

"So you think it was not Bonnier?"

She smiled. "I didn't say that. I was showing you that

there were dozens of people who could have felt that to get rid of my husband could be advantageous."

"But he wasn't political."

"Agreed. But he was a man of immense influence in this area. If he had lived people would have taken great notice of what he said. Inevitably he would have had views. The people in this area knew what he had done to fight the Germans and although he saw himself as a soldier they saw him as a brave and honest man. If you go down to the area by the cathedral in Périgueux you will find a small square named after him—Place Chaland. There are flowers around the little fountain all the year round. They put them there still."

"How did you meet him, madame?"

She smiled. "I was the courier between Bonnier and my husband and eventually I stayed with him. But it was for a very short time. He was captured soon after we were married."

"You knew he was English?"

"Of course." She leaned forward slightly. "Who told *you*?"

"Both Frenez and Bonnier seemed to take it for granted."

"Yes, he was English. But in many ways he was more French than the French. His mother was French and it had come from her, his love of France."

"Who do you think was the traitor?"

"I have no idea. It could have been anyone. They were nightmare times. Motives were mixed and people could succumb to pressure from the Germans. Physical threats, or threats to families."

"Your husband never suggested who he thought it might be."

"It's hard to explain now, but his life was too occupied to think of such things. He had no *time* to think of such things. And he didn't look for loyalty to himself. Action was what he set store by. Could his men do what he planned? That was the only thing."

"You must have seen him differently. More as a man than a leader."

"Both, perhaps. He was very young and I admired his single-mindedness and his courage. But he would have been a very gentle man in peace-time. He would have been a good husband, and a good father."

He looked at her face: "I'm sorry I have to talk about these things."

She shrugged: "It is all a long time ago. In a way I like to talk about him. I live here with Chantal but part of me belongs in that rough farm cottage at Puy Henry. There are very few people who actually remember him now."

"Did he ever talk about Bonnier or Communism?"

"He thought Bonnier was a good leader and a brave man but he recognized that Bonnier would have different interests. They used one another. He had no interest in any kind of politics and he would never have been interested in Communism."

"Do *you* think Bonnier could have betrayed him?"

She smiled. "Bonnier would have betrayed his own mother if Moscow had told him to. But I can't see him betraying Charles in Limoges at that stage of the war. Anyone who was fighting Germans successfully at that time was helping Moscow in a way. If my husband had lived I could see Bonnier as a relentless enemy. He hated Charles's indifference to politics. Couldn't understand why a man should risk his life ten times a day for a cause as indistinct as 'la belle France.' Of course if you really wanted to find out about the Limoges affair it would be easy enough."

"How?"

"The police in Limoges still have the Gestapo records. In the week that Charles was captured the SOE in this area made a concerted attack on the German counter-intelligence groups, and they never really recovered after that. Their records were captured in Limoges and Angoulême. I think in Périgueux they were destroyed when the buildings were fired."

Bailey looked at this pretty woman who had been part of all this history and he found it hard to imagine her as a Resistance worker. She turned her head to look at his face.

"What are you really trying to find out, Mr. Bailey?"

A variety of lies leapt into his mind but he couldn't bring himself to use them on this woman. She deserved better than that.

"I can't tell you, madame. It sounds silly but I don't really know what I'm looking for. I'm trying to trace the background of a man. When I've done my checking I'll be happy to explain properly."

She nodded and stood up. "Chantal and I will be taking lunch in half an hour, would you like to eat with us?"

She smiled before he answered because she could see the instant pleasure on his face.

"I should really like that, madame."

"Let's find that daughter of mine."

• • •

They had eaten in a small alcove, and the two ladies had been French and charming, and Bailey sensed that Madame Chaland was aware of his interest in the girl and was not antagonistic. And the girl had accepted his invitation to dinner at the hotel despite the fact that her mother had tactfully refused.

• • •

Bailey had left the hired car at a garage and walked to the Prefecture while they replaced the fan-belt.

Despite his credentials the police had checked with Paris before they would co-operate. And even then they had left an *inspecteur* with him as he sat in a small office looking at the Gestapo records for 1944. It took him an hour to find it. There was a pencilled number in the top right-hand corner and he asked the *inspecteur* if it had any significance. He leaned forward to look, and then, without further comment, the man said, "Yes, it means that that document has been photographed and microfilmed for SDECE and Deuxième Bureau records in Paris."

The paper was typed:

> Abwehr Aussenstelle, Limoges
> 13 Mai 1944
>
> The information received yesterday 12 Mai '44 from BONNIER has been evaluated as follows:

Informant BONNIER, MICHEL, aged 29, is suspected member of group of maquis operating in triangle LIMOGES—PÉRIGUEUX—ANGOULÉME. A number of reports have been received in the past eight months that he is leader of group or deputy leader.

His information is that CHALAND, CHARLES (See file 3491) will be in city area of LIMOGES tomorrow 14 Mai 1944. It is indicated that object of visit is to meet suspect FRENEZ, ANDRÉ (See file 3401 and special file 197). It is believed that CHALAND will travel by train. The information was passed to Milice sergeant at Brantôme by informant personally. Informant and Milice sergeant at same school.

It is now considered that motive of informant is internal conflicts of Resistance groups in this area. Informant is life-long member of Communist Party and information (See RSHA commentary 1304) is that all Communist-influenced Resistance groups have been instructed to establish with local population that they are sole active Resistance to German troops.

We now suspect that rivalry between CHALAND and BONNIER is sufficiently intense to cause BONNIER to seek elimination of CHALAND.

Attempts will be made to maintain this contact but caution has been advised.

Action will be taken by Gestapo against CHALAND but surveillance will be organized by Abwehr and SD. No action will be taken at this stage against suspect FRENEZ.

Signed Otto Paulsen (Hptn)

Distribution:
RSHA Berlin
OKW liaison
Gestapo Lyons
" Limoges
" Périgueux

Sicherheistdienst Limoges
" Lyons (information only)

• • •

They had eaten at a small restaurant facing the river and constantly intruding into his pleasure of being with the girl was the disturbing thought that made it seem more certain that the man who had sat talking with him and then had cut his throat was the girl's father. And he could imagine no reason why the man should have deserted the woman he loved and her unborn child. And why had he lived that strange, solitary life when he could have been with his family? He was sure that the answer lay with Bonnier.

"You look far away."

"I'm sorry. I was thinking about your mother and father and what it must have been like in those days."

"And what did you think?"

"That your mother must have found it a nightmare of anxiety, having a man who was in such continuous danger. And then when he was dead the nightmare would be all she had to remember and she would remember only small things about that man and the terrible times would become the good times. The time when he was alive and they were together."

"That's why she spends so much time at the cottage at Puy Henry. To remember."

"It's very romantic in many ways. Sort of old-fashioned. Knights in armour and their ladies."

The brown eyes looked at his face with affection. "Let's go up to the cottage for an hour and then you can take me home."

"Would your mother mind?"

"No. I think she rather likes you."

He opened his mouth to ask the question, and then closed it. He didn't dare risk the answer.

• • •

The big key was in the door and the girl opened the door and slid in her hand to find the light switch.

Bailey stood outside the cottage looking up at the sky. The stars looked big and near, and the moon was full and orange. He was aware that Chaland must have seen these same stars all those years ago, and it was almost the exact anniversary of when he had been captured. It couldn't have been Bonnier who had betrayed him that last night, because he had been captured too and sent to a German concentration camp. He turned and walked down the carpet of light from the open door.

"Chantal, where are you?"

He heard her voice from the small kitchen and he walked in. She was making coffee for them and she brushed her hair over her shoulder with one hand as she turned to look at him.

"I wondered where you were."

"Let's sit at the table and drink our coffee." As she set out the coffee cups and poured out for them both he could look at her face. She was so beautiful that it hurt and the movements of her hands had the same grace as when she had played the piano.

"White or black?" And when she looked up to get his answer she looked away at the intensity of his look.

"White, please."

They had barely sat down before she spoke. "You were going to ask me at the restaurant if I liked you. Yes?"

"Yes." He found it hard to keep his eyes on her face as he waited.

"I do like you. But I don't want you to like me too much."

"Is there someone else?"

She put down the small cup and leaned forward with her arms on the table.

"There are other men who like me. Yes. But there is nobody who is special to me. I am single-minded about my music and emotional ties would hinder me."

"But you don't mind that I care about you?"

The sweeping black eyelashes came up and her eyes were concerned. "It would not be fair to you. There would be so little in return."

He put his hand across the table to touch her hand and she smiled as his fingers covered hers.

"But I could write to you and maybe see you sometimes."

"Tell me what it is that makes you like me."

He smiled despite the tension inside him. "It's not possible to say, Chantal. You're beautiful, but you will know that. I just like everything about you. I feel I want to protect you."

"From what?"

He shrugged. "From unpleasant things. Life, and all that."

Her fingers squeezed his gently. "You're a nice man and I *do* like you, but I don't want to hurt you."

"I'll risk that."

"OK."

"Will you play something for me when I take you home?"

She laughed. "Of course. What shall I play?"

"Something specially for me."

"I'll do that. Let me show you over the cottage." She stood up. "They lived here for a short time you know and Maman and I lived here for two years when I was a baby."

They explored the few bare rooms and she washed up the coffee things as he stood watching. And then she was turning the key in the cottage door as he stood in the small garden. Everywhere smelt of autumn, a lush, rotting sweetness. A dampness that called for warmth and log fires.

Her arm slid in his and they walked to the small gate in the low wall. And as he held it open for her she turned towards him, her face upturned in the moonlight. His arms went round her and his mouth was gentle on her soft lips. When she drew back he said, "Try and love me some day."

She looked towards the dark cottage where the moon made the white walls grey. And then she looked back up at his face. "Would it help if we made love?"

There was a moment's silence then he said: "If *we* did, not if just I did." She nodded and took his hand and they walked slowly back to the cottage, and upstairs to the small bed where her mother had once sat watching Chaland's face as he slept.

He had been aware that she knew what men would want from her body and that her love-making was as experienced as his own, but the pleasure and excitement from having her was *now* and it crowded out his feeling that although he could have her body he would never possess her heart.

It was after midnight when they were back at the house in

Brantôme. The lights were still on but there was no sign of her mother.

She sat down at the piano and lifted the lid. He leaned on the piano as her hands stretched and her fingers touched the keyboard. And as she played he recognized the little melody by Chaminade and the words:

"Plaisir d'amour
ne dure q'un moment
Chagrin d'amour
Dure toute la vie."

When the soft notes fell away he looked at her and said softly: "I love you, Chantal."

She looked back at him. "I know you do. But you must go."

"I'm going to Paris tomorrow. Can I see you when I come back?"

"Have you not finished down here?"

"I won't ever be finished down here. No matter what happens."

She closed the lid of the piano and walked with him to the door. She stood and watched as he walked to the gate, and that had made him happy. When he waved she waved back and then closed the door.

Chapter Twelve

He had phoned Bonnier's office three times. Bonnier was out until early evening.

At six-thirty he was put through.

"Bonnier."

"M'sieur Bonnier, this is Bailey. I spoke with you a few days ago about M'sieur Chaland. Could I see you again?"

"I'm sorry, my friend, I've given you all the help I can."

"It wouldn't take much time."

"I'm sorry, I cannot help you further."

There was a pause and Bailey said slowly, "I've seen the Gestapo records at Limoges."

"For Christ's sake . . ." Bonnier stopped and there was a long silence. Then: "Where are you, Bailey?"

"Hotel Normandie, Rue des Capucines."

"I'll come round and see you in an hour."

• • •

Bonnier had seemed huge in the small hotel bar and he had walked in as if he owned the place. He threw his wet raincoat down and turned to the waiter: "Bring some whisky. Scotch. A bottle." He then glared at Bailey.

"Right, say what you've got to say."

"I checked the Gestapo records at Limoges for 1944."

"And?"

"And I saw the report that you had tipped them off about Chaland."

"That doesn't mean a thing, comrade. Could have been planted by the Germans."

"I don't think that photocopies for SDECE and other organizations in Paris would have been sent if the authorities had any doubts."

"Those bastards would do anything to embarrass the Party. We can have them destroyed. We have people throughout the government."

"But a lot of people have seen the records."

"So what. They're employees of the State. If they shot their mouths off we should see that they lost their jobs."

"I'm not an employee of the State."

Bonnier's big hands were gripping the table as if he would tear the room to pieces.

"What is it you want?"

"The truth about Chaland."

"I've told you all I know."

Bailey shook his head: "Not by a long way, Bonnier. I want the whole story."

The big man turned as the waiter came with the whisky and glasses, and then turned back to look at Bailey, waiting until the barman had left.

"What is it you want to know?"

"What happened to Chaland?"

"How the hell should I know?"

"I can find out in other ways. *Figaro* and *Le Monde* would be glad of the story. There would be an enquiry and what happened to Chaland would come out at the trial."

"Nobody would believe it."

Bailey's smile was grim: "You know that's not so, Bonnier. They'd believe it even if it wasn't true."

Bonnier reached forward and poured himself a whisky and

topped up the glass with a small amount of water. He looked over his glass at Bailey as he sipped.

"I hear you've been in Périgueux sniffing around his family."

Bailey stayed silent and Bonnier sipped slowly at his drink. He leaned forward and put down the empty glass. As he leaned back he said: "Did you get it up the sweet Chantal? I heard she was taking all sizes when she was at the Académie, black ones and brown ones too."

Bailey didn't respond but Bonnier smiled as he saw the white knuckles and the slow flush of anger. He went on.

"Those two aren't going to like what comes out of an enquiry."

"There doesn't have to be an enquiry, Bonnier. Just tell me what happened. I know part of the story."

Bonnier smiled. "Don't bluff me, Bailey. I've been calling bluffs all my life."

"Call me, then."

"OK. You tell me your part and if you're right I'll tell you the rest on one condition."

"What's the condition?"

"That it's between us, not for anyone else."

Bailey shook his head. "No can do, Bonnier. No conditions, just common sense."

"Tell me what you know."

"I'll tell you what. Enough for you to know that I'm not bluffing. Your little friend Siwecki has been using an art gallery on the Left Bank as a dead-letter drop. And he makes contact with an Englishman there. But he hasn't seen the Englishman for nearly five months now."

Bonnier had listened intently with his big head on one side like a blackbird listening for worms in a lawn. When Bailey stopped talking Bonnier looked down at the carpet between them and after a few moments he looked up at Bailey and said quietly: "OK. Let's talk."

Bonnier leaned his head back against the top of the chair and closed his eyes. His massive chest rose and fell with his breathing and Bailey waited in silence. Finally Bonnier started talking.

"Chaland and I were caught on the same night. Nobody

betrayed us, we made our own mistakes, and we killed a lot of Germans before they got us. I was taken in Périgueux and Chaland was taken at the Gestapo house on the other side of the river. I was taken to that house and so were the others who had been caught. There were about nine or ten of us in all.

"They had been after Chaland for months and they knew who he was as soon as they got him. The Allies were driving across France and the Germans in France were desperate to keep the Resistance off the backs of their troops moving from the South as reinforcements. So they were in a hurry to round up everyone in Chaland's group, which was the biggest in France. There were maquis troops far bigger but we couldn't do what the likes of Chaland could do.

"We heard Chaland screaming all through the night and the next day. It was almost non-stop. Devereux and I were given the cold bath treatment but their hearts weren't in it. We didn't know much and they knew it. Chaland was the one. The screams stopped in the middle of the second night and we knew he was either dead or unconscious and they couldn't revive him.

"The next day we were all rounded up and taken on trucks to the railway station and we heard from one of the guards that they were shipping us to Germany. Chaland was on a stretcher, and the rest of us had shackles on our feet and handcuffs. And a chain round our necks attached to the handcuffs and the shackles. The chains weighed a bloody ton. When they put us on the railway wagons Chaland was chained to me. You couldn't even go for a crap without the guy you were chained to going with you. It was just sadism. He was in a coma all the time. He looked dead already.

"We were in the wagons for two nights and three days. The train was attacked by the RAF once. The guards took cover and left us chained up.

"On the second night Chaland was delirious. Talking in English to a guy named Fredericks. Then he was sending messages to him telling him that the Germans had found out he was married to Sabine and that she was pregnant. And they'd threatened to bring her in and let them rape her in front of him, and then they'd cut her open. So he told them what they wanted to know about the three reseaux under his command. He'd given them names and code-names, addresses, arms caches, everything. And he was begging them to warn his people. He was still alive when we got to the camp, at Natzweiler. It was a miracle. The party members fixed for me to become a "Kapo" and a few weeks later I got Chaland transferred to the hospital. By then it was nearly over. The Americans and the British were over the Rhine and the party was sending orders to our people at the camp to get Chaland out.

"By then he was conscious for a few hours every day and I got him out of the camp to a party member's house. I stayed with him until the surrender and somebody came from the party HQ at Dresden and took over.

"When he was fit they told him they knew what he had done and he tried to kill himself.

"He was taken to a mental hospital in the East Zone and they told him he would be exposed if he didn't work for the Party.

"They sent me to talk to him a few weeks after that. It was like talking to a ghost. He looked an old man. I told him he was the local hero in Périgueux and that his wife was being well looked after and that if he went back we should make public what had happened and that would be the end of all of them. At least forty people were killed by the Germans because he talked.

"In the end he was sent back to England by the Russians. They fixed false documents and gave him the money to set up a small business. I was out of the picture by then. He was a courier and his contact in Paris was Siwecki."

Although it was not much more than Bailey had suspected, the room seemed dark and cold as he sat there. The details were too terrible to contemplate. His mind could encompass the bald facts but when it imagined Chaland's experiences it was too much.

He looked over at Bonnier. "Not a nice story, Bonnier."

"They were not nice times, comrade."

"They still aren't."

Bonnier sat in silence looking at Bailey. Waiting for him to react.

Bailey said: "Does anyone else know Chaland's background? Does Siwecki know?"

"Siwecki's just a messenger boy. It was all a long time ago, my friend. It's probably on some KGB file in Moscow but I'd guess it's got dust on it by now. He wasn't that important even in the early stages. He was just a useful tool."

"D'you regret any of this, Bonnier?"

The big man shifted in the chair, shrugging. "Individuals are unimportant, Bailey. Twenty million Russians died in the war. What is one man against that?"

"And the woman and the child?"

"They have survived, my friend. Better than they deserved. He *talked*, comrade, he was a traitor. Forty people died so that a woman could stay alive and have a child."

Bailey looked at him: "So we both keep our little secrets. Is that how it should be?"

Bonnier stood up, smiling: "A good British compromise. That's what your people say, isn't it."

And he had reached for his raincoat and walked to the door. As he stood there he said, smiling, "You'll get anything you want from the little girl now."

And in that moment Bailey realized that it wasn't all over yet.

• • •

Siwecki was sitting with the girl in the gallery as Bailey walked in. There was a bottle of wine on the green baize card-table that held the visitors' book.

The girl seemed pleased to see him, and as he sipped white wine with them he invited them both to dinner. But they said that it wasn't possible for them to accept. They were going to dinner with a prospective client.

Bailey looked around for a chair and finding none he leaned back against the wall between two big paintings.

Siwecki was turning over the pages of a newspaper and it was a second before Bailey's question went home.

"What's happened to Walters, Andrei?"

Then his head came up fast, his mouth open. "What was that?"

"What's happened to Walters?"

Siwecki glanced quickly at the girl and then back to Bailey.

"Who the devil is Walters?"

"The Englishman. The KGB courier from London."

Siwecki folded the paper slowly and carefully. He looked at the girl. "I'll see you later, Monique. I'll call you."

Bailey's foot came down on Siwecki's. "Don't go, Andrei. Just answer one question."

Siwecki hesitated. "What is it?"

"All I want to know is how many times a year did he come to France?"

"Every month."

"Did he ever go elsewhere in France other than Paris?"

"Sometimes he did."

"Where did he go?"

"He never said, but I had him followed once and he went to a small place called Brantôme. He drove down by car. Parked it opposite a house and waited for half an hour and then drove back again to Paris."

"Anybody come out of the house?"

"Two women."

"What did they do?"

"Nothing. They walked to a restaurant but he didn't follow."

"Any idea why he did this?"

"No idea at all. Seemed crazy to me."

Bailey looked at the girl's shocked face. "Don't worry, Monique, there's no problem."

And he turned and left the gallery without looking back.

• • •

He had used the SDECE facilities to check Bonnier's movements. Bonnier's office had said that he was not there and was not expected back that night. SDECE had his unlisted home number and there was no reply. And Bailey knew by instinct where Bonnier would be.

Bailey paid his plane fare in dollars to get quick service, and the other passengers for the plane to Bordeaux were already on board. Bonnier was not among them. He wouldn't have a need for that sort of hurry.

An hour and a half later the plane put down at Bordeaux and Bailey booked a hire car at the airport. Half an hour later he was heading for Périgueux and an hour later he was on the bridge at Brantôme. He parked the car fifty yards from the house and walked to the big iron gate. There was one light on in the house. He was breathing heavily as he pressed the bell.

It was the girl who answered the door and he said, "Where's your mother, Chantal?"

"She's gone to the cottage."

"When did she leave?"

"Five minutes ago."

"Why?"

"There was a phone call."

"From Paris?"

"No, local."

"Did she say who it was?"

"No. She wouldn't talk about it. She seemed upset or frightened, and that's not like her. I said I would go with her but she got very agitated and begged me not to interfere. I'm so frightened. What's going on?"

"Get your coat quickly and come with me, we must get up there at once."

• • •

As they swung off the main road and found the track up to Puy Henry the car swayed and lurched across the rutted surface, and when they got to the new piece of track Bailey pulled the car into the side of the hill. As he got out he said: "Stay here, Chantal. I'll be back soon."

He ran up the path and heard the girl close the car door behind him. At the crest of the hill he saw two cars. One was Madame Chaland's Fiat, and the other was a post-office van. He put his hand on both radiators and they were both painfully hot. The van was hissing steam from under the bonnet.

He scrambled over the low wall and ran crouching to the

side of the cottage. The curtains were drawn but he could see part of the room. The woman sat at the table, her head on her arms, and he could hear her sobs over Bonnier's angry voice.

". . . And I promise you, madame, that if he talks I shall talk too and your life in Brantôme will be finished, there will be . . ."

Bailey shoved open the door of the cottage. Bonnier was standing at the end of the table, his eyes bulging and his face red with anger. Bonnier's hand was half-raised, his mouth open in surprise as he saw Bailey. His anger was diverted to Bailey and he walked round the table to stand hand on hips, with his head thrust forward aggressively.

"What do you want, sonny boy?"

"I want you to leave, Bonnier. Now."

The bloodshot eyes glared at Bailey and a clenched fist waved in front of his face.

"I don't trust you, you English bastard."

"And I don't trust you Bonnier, what . . ."

And Bailey saw the big fist swinging for his face. He caught it with both hands as Bonnier's left fist took him in the ribs. He swung Bonnier round and put his shoulder to his massive chest. The impact sent the sixteen-stone man back against the wall, but his free arm came round and his strong fingers scrabbled to find the pressure point behind Bailey's ear. But despite Bonnier's animal strength he was too old, too out of condition and his breath came in great gasps, as he pushed Bailey back against the table. Bailey released Bonnier's right hand and reaching for his throat sent Bonnier back against the wall. There was a sickening noise like a coconut cracking and Bonnier's hands fell to his side. The bulging eyes quivered then closed and Bonnier's large body collapsed and slid down the wall, his feet tangling in the chair by the table as he fell.

Bailey's fingers searched the big hairy wrist for a pulse but there was none. He bent to put his ear to the barrel chest but there was no heart-beat. Bonnier was dead. His legs shaking, he stood up with one hand against the wall to keep his balance.

Bailey turned to look at the woman, her face distraught, her hair awry. He leaned against the table to recover his breath. When he could speak he said, "I want you to go to your car, madame. Just down the hill is my car. Chantal is there, and I want you to take her back to your house. Tell her nothing about what has happened here. Nothing at all. What Bonnier told you was lies. It was to protect himself from me."

The tanned face looked grey and old, and her hands trembled as she tried to stand up.

"Don't move, Maman."

And he had gone to the kitchen and soaked a cloth under the running tap.

She sat like a child as he gently wiped her face, and her lips quivered as she remembered wiping her husband's torn face when he came back from Nolke's offices. But she slowly recovered and stood up.

"Try hard for Chantal's sake, Maman."

She nodded and walked slowly to the door. A little later he heard her car start and he looked back to where Bonnier lay. There was a trickle of blood from his ear. When he lifted one eyelid the eye was turned back up into the head and the eyelid stayed open when he released it.

It took an hour to get Bonnier to the van and twenty minutes to get him in place on the right-hand front seat.

He had seen the hose looped across two pegs on the kitchen wall and he carried it to the back of the van. The bore was too small when he tried to get it over the exhaust pipe, but it was a tight fit inside the pipe.

In Brantôme the streets were deserted and he glanced at his watch. It was one o'clock. As he drove through Périgueux he saw a signpost pointing to Bordeaux and in the opposite direction it pointed to Brive-la-Gaillarde. He had never heard of the place but he headed the car in that direction.

He had done fifteen kilometres before he turned up a lane on the left-hand side of the road. He drove the car slowly into the ditch, so that it leaned almost at its point of balance. Bonnier's body slid like a huge carnival figure behind the wheel and he walked along the ditch to a small culvert and forced out one of the old bricks. When he had stuffed the hose up the exhaust pipe, twisting it to drive it right home, he trailed the hose to the front of the car. He leaned over and started the engine and balanced the brick against the accelerator. He pushed the hose under the car door where it was bent, and closed the door.

Thirty-three years before, Bonnier and Chaland had ambushed the German ambulance at this same spot where he and his men had hidden the German army motorcycles.

Chapter Thirteen

At Brive-la-Gaillarde Bailey found a telephone kiosk and dialled the Brantôme number. Madame Chaland answered and he described where he was and asked her to pick him up. She sounded back in control of herself and she said she could be there in half an hour.

Bailey walked back down the road that led to Périgueux and sat in the shelter of a hedge while he waited. His mind was a storm of conflicting thoughts. He tried to recall every word that he had said to Walters. He remembered the comparatively mild pressure that he had applied by asking the purpose of the visit to France. The man would not have known which visit he was referring to, and with all those years of sacrifice about to be set at nought he must have decided in a few seconds to kill himself to prevent an exposure that he felt could have destroyed the security of his wife and child. The man had shown every kind of courage there was until his wife was threatened. And because of that single hostage to fate the hero became a traitor. She had been the only person in the world he had. The choice would have driven the bravest man to the edge of treachery, and, beaten to a pulp, his resistance must have been minimal. He remembered reading in one of the SOE files of a Frenchman and his wife who had seen their two young children killed in front of them by the Germans to make them give their comrades' names. How did you live for the rest of your life with the screams of fear and the terrible sight. It must be easier to betray those whose torture and death you wouldn't witness.

He saw the car lights approaching slowly and he stepped out into the road. As he slid into the seat he said, "Turn here, don't go into Brive."

He waited as she criss-crossed the road and then said: "How is Chantal?"

"I think she is confused and worried, but I have told her nothing. Absolutely nothing."

"Was it Bonnier himself who phoned?"

"Yes."

"I want to ask you to forget everything that happened tonight. You never saw Bonnier."

"He may have told others that he was seeing me."

"He won't have, you can be sure of that. He had good reason not to."

"He said you might try to expose him. Something from his past. What was it all about?"

"I told him something I knew to get some information I wanted from him. There was no question of exposing him. He was scared, he wanted to put pressure on you so that there would be pressure on me."

"Was it true what he said about Charles? That he was a traitor?"

"You must know that it wasn't true. He must have risked his life dozens of times for the sake of other people."

"Bonnier said it was to save me."

"I told you. Bonnier was scared. Frightened men can be desperate. It was a crude attempt at blackmail."

"Where is he now?"

"He's dead, and I want you to forget tonight for my sake. Please, Maman."

"You love Chantal don't you?"

"What makes you say that?"

"The way you speak to her. Your voice changes. You're a man who is very sure of himself. But when you are with her you are on edge. Wanting to please her and uncertain how to do it."

"I must have looked very transparent."

"Not at all. Vulnerable, yes, but not transparent. But I am her mother so I'm bound to notice these things."

"And what do you think?"

"About you and Chantal?"

"Yes."

"You will have adjustments to make to each other. You'll have to tempt her out of that cloud of music and she will have to give you the confidence you will need with her."

He was silent as they entered Brantôme and she spoke again. "I'll help you both all I can."

He shivered as he said: "Will you take me up to Puy Henry? My hire car is still up there. Can I stay up there to sleep?"

"Of course. Or use the spare room at the house."

"Will you stay and have some coffee with me, Maman?"

"Yes, of course."

She stopped at his car and he drove it up the hill, following her.

When she brought in the coffee they sat at the table sipping slowly in silence. Finally he looked at her as he spoke.

"I want to stay here, Maman, for a few days. I want to see what happens about Bonnier. If it all dies down I shall go back to London. If there are problems I shall stay on and deal with them. I don't want you or Chantal to be involved in any way."

"You'll see Chantal before you go back?"

He sighed and shook his head. "If she ever talks about me will you tell her that you know for certain that I love her."

"Why don't you tell her yourself?"

"It isn't possible, Maman, after tonight. I can't explain, it's too confused. I'll sort it out all right but it will be best for you and Chantal to see no more of me."

There were long moments of silence and then she said softly: "Do two men have to do that?"

His voice was low as he shook his head.

"Don't say that, Maman. Don't think it. But I love her so much." And the tears streamed down his face.

She stood beside him, her arms across his bent shoulders to comfort him, and she remembered how long ago she had comforted another young man in the small room in Périgueux.

She bent down and kissed his cheek and he heard the door close behind her as she left.

• • •

There was nothing in the morning paper but in the evening paper there was a brief report.

Périgueux

Prominent Communist found dead

Early this morning the body was found of Michel Bonnier, a member of the Communist Party's main committee. It was discovered by farmer Georges Yves Bilbaud, in a post-office vehicle in a minor road off the Brive-Périgueux road.

Inspecteur Tassy at police HQ in Périgueux stated that the authorities are investigating all possibilities, including murder. Michel Bonnier was a leader of the maquisards in the area during the war and in certain quarters it is suggested that there may be political aspects to this crime.

After the war M. Bonnier was an important functionary in the Post-Office Union and there are reports that he left Paris yesterday evening in the Bordeaux mail-plane.

Maître Frenez of Limoges who knew Bonnier well during Resistance days told our reporter,

"Michel Bonnier was a fine leader of men, and his record in the war-time Resistance was second to none. Although I did not share his political ideology I respected the man, and I view with apprehension what appears to be a back-lash of violent political action. It would be well for M. Bonnier's colleagues in Paris to take note that violence from the Left can induce violence from other quarters."

M. Bonnier was unmarried, but left a married sister who lives in Angoulême.

Agence France–Presse

• • •

There had been nothing to connect Bonnier's death at Brive-la-Gaillarde with any particular person in the area and over the next seven days the news items were briefer and indicated that a verdict would be brought in at the inquest of murder by persons unknown.

On the last evening Bailey had dialled the SDECE number in Paris. His contact had checked the police reports on Bonnier and had phoned back. The autopsy had indicated that Bonnier had not died from carbon-monoxide poisoning as was first suspected but from cerebral lesions from a blow to the head. There were a hundred theories but no suspects, and neither SDECE nor the police were in mourning.

• • •

That evening Bailey had parked the car well away from the Chalands' house and had walked slowly in the darkness in the hope that he might see the girl. And he knew, with a heavy heart, that Walters must have done the same over the years, hoping to see from a distance the woman he loved and their child. And sitting in the lonely flat in Putney checking the child's progress in the much thumbed Dr. Spock.

There were lights on in the house but nobody emerged. It was almost one o'clock in the morning when he crossed the road and stood at the gate, his aching head touching the cold of the metal Croix de Lorraine. Then he walked slowly back to the car and drove to the airport at Bordeaux.

The buildings were almost empty and he waited to catch the early plane to London.

• • •

At Sloane Square he had turned, gone down King's Road and was almost at Putney Bridge before his tired brain realized that that was no longer home. He turned in a side-street and went back to Sloane Square and up to Kensington High Street.

The flat smelled of dust and stale air. There was a small pile of mail in the hall and he gathered it up and walked through to the kitchen.

He ripped open the envelopes as he waited for the kettle to boil, and when he had made the coffee he read through the letters.

There was a final demand for payment of the electricity bill, a coded Home Office payslip showing a salary transfer to his account at Coutts. A coloured postcard of Albufeira from a girl-friend and a library reminder for two overdue books.

There was a letter from his solicitors:

> Dear Mr. Bailey,
>
> We have to inform you that we have heard from Mrs. Jane Bailey's solicitors, Messrs. Mason, Lygon and Porter, that they are applying to the Court for a variation of the order giving you access to the child of the marriage Jonathan Nicholas.
>
> We understand that the application is to vary the order so that access is completely denied. The particulars we have received are by no means satisfactory and we have asked for further and better particulars. However, the essence of the application is that "arrangements for access are continually cancelled at short notice and Mrs. Bailey's relationship with the child is being undermined by the father's criticism of her to her son." It is claimed that this is causing the child considerable distress.
>
> We were not able to contact you by telephone

despite several attempts, and as the hearing is put down for the 27th of this mouth we should appreciate you contacting us urgently with a view to a meeting to discuss the matter. We assume you will want to oppose this application.

Yours faithfully,
Richard Walker
Parish, Walker & Co

• • •

To: Chief Superintendent Murphy—Special Branch
From: Commander Bailey, N.
Subject: *Walters, J.F.—Security Suspect*

Following the request from FO liaison I have investigated the background of the above.

Despite intensive investigations in the UK and overseas I have been unable to establish the true identity of the subject, or find any connection with any foreign intelligence service beyond the original information (See P File/49731).